DEKOK AND
MURDER IN ECSTASY

"DeKok" Books by A.C. Baantjer:

Published in the United States:
Murder in Amsterdam
DeKok and the Sunday Strangler
DeKok and the Corpse on Christmas Eve
DeKok and the Somber Nude
DeKok and the Dead Harlequin
DeKok and the Sorrowing Tomcat
DeKok and the Disillusioned Corpse
DeKok and the Careful Killer
DeKok and the Romantic Murder
DeKok and the Dying Stroller
DeKok and the Corpse at the Church Wall
DeKok and the Dancing Death
DeKok and the Naked Lady
DeKok and the Brothers of the Easy Death
DeKok and the Deadly Accord
DeKok and Murder in Seance
DeKok and Murder in Ecstasy
DeKok and Murder on the Menu

Available soon from InterContinental Publishing:
DeKok and the Begging Death
DeKok and the Geese of Death
DeKok and Murder by Melody
DeKok and Death of a Clown
DeKok and Variations on Murder
DeKok and Murder by Installments
DeKok and Murder on Blood Mountain
DeKok and the Dead Lovers
DeKok and the Mask of Death
DeKok and the Corpse by Return
DeKok and Murder in Bronze
DeKok and the Deadly Warning
DeKok and Murder First Class
DeKok and the Vendetta
DeKok and Murder Depicted
DeKok and Dance Macabre
DeKok and the Disfiguring Death
DeKok and the Devil's Conspiracy
DeKok and the Duel at Night
and more . . .

DeKok
and
Murder in Ecstasy

by

BAANTJER

translated from the Dutch by H.G. Smittenaar

INTERCONTINENTAL PUBLISHING

ISBN 1 881164 16 0

Printing History:
    1st Dutch printing: 1982
    17th Dutch printing: 1997

    1st American edition: 1998

Typography: Monica S. Rozier
Cover by: Rosemary Boyd of Document Design, Laguna Beach, CA
Manufactured by: BookCrafters, Fredericksburg, VA

Library of Congress Cataloging-in-Publication Data

Baantjer, A. C.
    [De Cock en de moord in extase. English]
    DeKok and murder in ecstasy / by Baantjer ; translated from the Dutch by H.G. Smittenaar.
       p.   cm.
    ISBN 1-881164-16-0 (alk. paper)
    I. Smittenaar, H. G.
    PT5881.12.A2D56413 1998
    839.3'1364—dc21   97–42994
                                                     CIP

DeKok
and
Murder in Ecstasy

1

"Idiot! Crazy bastard!"

Richard Sloten pulled the ski mask off his face with an angry gesture. His face was red and his green eyes spat fire.

"Was that necessary?" he roared. "If that guy dies, we'll have a murder on our conscience!"

Peter ignored him. He drove the sleek Alfa Romeo out of Wibaut Street and manoeuvred recklessly past a long line of cars that were stalled, bumper to bumper, waiting for a traffic light. He ignored the light and crossed within inches of oncoming traffic from the side street, another quick turn and he raced toward Amstel Station. Not until they reached the highway out of town, did he glance aside.

"He recognized me," said Peter curtly.

"Who?"

"The driver of the armored car."

Richard turned toward his partner.

"Dammit, that's no reason to *kill* him . . . to shoot him, just like that."

Peter snorted.

"What would you have me do?" he asked bitingly. "Just wait for the cops to come after us right away?" He gestured with a thumb over his shoulder, pointing at the stack of linen bags on the back seat of the car. "Then what would we do with the loot? Nothing . . . absolutely nothing! We'd get to turn it in, have it confiscated more likely . . . and we'd be behind bars."

Richard Sloten shook his head.

"It's your own stupid mistake. Why in hell didn't you keep your mask on?"

Peter gripped the steering wheel more securely.

"I was sweating," he said calmly. "Those bags of money were heavy and that woolen thing scratched my neck. I can't stand that. Besides . . . it obstructed my view."

It was Richard's turn to snort.

"Idiot! I should never have hooked up with you. My mother warned me about you. You're too nervous for this work . . . too quick with the trigger . . . you maniac!"

Peter grinned. It was a strange, twisted grin that gave his handsome face a diabolic expression.

"For the time being . . . for the time being you have a lot of money because of this *maniac*. A lot of money, yessir. Just think what you can do with it all." He paused, glanced at his partner. "The other car is in Dovecote?"

Richard nodded.

"On a quiet stretch of Winken Road. There's a grassy area nearby. You can park right next to it and it'll be easy to reload."

"Tank full?"

Richard reacted sharply.

"Of course the tank is full, you idiot." The anger about the unexpected shooting of the driver bubbled up again. He did not like violence. He had always avoided it and all his crimes had been committed without violence of any kind. The police only knew him as a petty criminal. They were supposed to hold up the armored car . . . daringly and suddenly, but without violence . . . of any kind. They had agreed to that and each swore to the agreement. Peter's revolver was to be used as an inducement . . .

nothing else. A compelling inducement not to be resisted, but the weapon was *not* to be used, under any circumstances.

Peter drove the car to its limits. Richard's spluttering left him unmoved. He had no use for sentimentality. He had his own ideas about how to commit a crime. Obstacles were to be removed at all costs . . . even at the cost of a few bullets.

He looked at Richard, who stared out of the window with a pale face. Less than an hour ago he had believed the boy to be a good partner, a trustworthy mate to help him get rich quick. He grinned to himself. Apparently he had been mistaken. The boy had a weak chin.

Near the town of Dovecote he took a right, crossed the bridge and turned into Winken Road.

"What sort of car is it?"

"A blue Jaguar."

"You tried it?"

Richard nodded with a stubborn look.

"The thing flies. There isn't a Porsche that can keep up with it, souped up, or not." Richard was referring to the Netherlands State Police, who patrol in Porsches.

"Changed the plates?"

Richard turned violently.

"We agreed on that, didn't we?" he barked.

Peter raised a soothing hand.

"I'm just checking. Just to be sure. After all, I've never worked with *you* either."

Richard took a deep breath.

"I," he said hoarsely, "I am used to keeping my promises. Not like you . . . you shoot . . . ."

He stopped suddenly and sat up straight. His Adam's apple bobbed up and down. "Drive on," he said. His voice broke. "Drive on . . . there's a cop."

"Where?"

"Next to the Jaguar."

Peter cursed. A tic pulsated on his cheek. He changed gears and with a roaring engine they raced past the cop. The cop, who was standing next to the Jaguar with a notebook in his hands, looked up in surprise.

Richard peered through the rear window.

"They saw us," he panted. "They know the tag number of this car, of course."

Peter cursed again. Long and hard. With an intense expression he increased the speed of the Alfa Romeo. He barely missed a large truck that was exiting an industrial park. With a wild, but controlled movement, he avoided a skid.

At the end of Winken Road, the six white towers of Bilmer Jail loomed up against a gray sky.

Peter ignored the view. He kept his eyes on the road. Every muscle was tense, every nerve ending alert. His sharply chiseled face looked like a steel mask.

"Are they following?"

Richard looked back, the fright of the near-skid still in his eyes.

"I can hear the siren, but I don't see anything." His voice shook. "We're far ahead."

Just before the steep walls of Bilmer Jail, Peter pulled the red Alfa through a sharp curve and changed direction. The chassis groaned and the tires howled. The noise increased as they hit the cobble stones of the old farmer's road toward the highway.

Richard yelled out above the noise.

"Where are you going?"

"There's a short-cut up ahead. From there to Dovecote Way and then back to Winken Road."

Richard looked at him with amazement in his eyes.

"Back to Winken Road?"

Peter nodded.

"To the Jaguar."

"You're crazy."

Peter grinned and the satanic look on his face was again evident.

"I'm not crazy," he said, spitting out the words. "You'll find out." It sounded scornful and with a hint of a threat. "If we can stay out of sight, it's our only chance. Within minutes this entire area will be crawling with cops, all of them on the look-out for a red Alfa Romeo." His face relaxed. "And they're welcome to find it . . . but without us." He waved toward the rear seat. "And without the money."

Richard shook his head in despair.

"The Jaguar has been seen. You saw that yourself. The cop was writing down the numbers."

Peter nodded.

"But before they've realized the Jaguar is gone, we're long gone as well." He glanced aside. "How about the keys?"

Richard rummaged in a coat pocket and held up the keys.

"We'll have to change cars once more," he commented with a worried look on his face.

Peter did not answer. He whipped the Alfa over the bad pavement of Dovecote Way. About a hundred yards before the bridge he stopped on the shoulder.

"Go get the Jaguar," he ordered.

Richard Sloten opened the door hesitantly.

"What if there are cops around?"

Peter's face flushed red.

"There won't be any cops," he growled angrily. "You saw that yourself. They're behind us."

Richard closed the car door and ran toward the Jaguar. He was back in less than two minutes and pulled up next to the Alfa Romeo.

Gasping with the weight, they heaved the money bags from one car into the other. In the distance police sirens could be heard clearly. The sound acted as a spur to their shattered nerves as cold sweat beaded their forehead. When the last bag had been transferred, they jumped in the Jaguar. Peter pulled over the wheel and gravel spewed out from behind as he left a long streak of rubber on the road.

* * *

Detective-Inspector DeKok of the Amsterdam Municipal Police (Homicide), attached to the busy Warmoes Street station, hissed between his teeth.

"Three million . . . dear me . . . I've been known to put a lot less than that in the collection plate on Sunday." He looked at Vledder, his assistant, partner and friend, who sat at his own desk next to his. "What kind of money is it, Dick?"

The young Inspector pushed his lower lip out as he kept one eye on his computer screen and another on a stack of notes he had taken over the phone.

"Nice money. Used currency . . . no records of the numbers and all in small denominations. Easy to spend . . . no problem whatsoever. The receipts from a number of department stores and supermarkets in town."

DeKok nodded his understanding.

"And the driver is dead?"

Vledder looked serious.

"One of the robbers put two bullets in his head. They had cut off the armored car on Gelder Quay, near New Market."

"Why would they kill him?"

Vledder shrugged.

"I don't know. According to witnesses, there was no reason. The man was disarmed and he did not resist. He was facing the truck, hands in the air."

DeKok's eyebrows flickered. Vledder watched, fascinated, as the body parts seemed to become detached from the forehead and take on a life of their own. DeKok's eyebrows were often the subject of heavy speculation. There were some who were convinced they were not part of the body, that it was all a trick. Others wondered how DeKok managed the extraordinary gymnastics with his eyebrows. The fact remained that DeKok's eyebrows seemed capable of actions more easily associated with the tendrils of an insect, than with the human anatomy. It also seemed a fact that DeKok himself was utterly oblivious to the acrobatics performed on his forehead.

The display took only a few seconds and, as usual, was gone before an onlooker could be sure they had seen what they thought they saw.

"And then he was gunned down?"

Vledder came back to the present with a start.

"Yes. The robber made a point of coming back. The money had already been transferred to the get-away car. According to witnesses, it was murder, cold-blooded murder . . . senseless."

"Are the witnesses any use?"

Vledder shook his head, making some adjustments on his keyboard. He glanced at the screen before he answered.

"All were very vague. No useful description among them."

DeKok came from behind his desk and started to pace up and down the large, crowded detective room. With subconscious ease he avoided obstacles in his path and his mind shut out the noise in the room. As he paced his thoughts became more ordered. After a while he stopped in front of Vledder's desk.

"What's the name of the victim?"

Vledder knew without consulting his computer.

"Martin ... Martin Muller, twenty-seven, married with three children."

"Does he have a record?"

"No," answered Vledder. "Has been with the firm for years and is a trusted employee. Also, he's a good husband and provider, irreproachable conduct. He has no police record and his finances are in order."

DeKok bit his lower lip.

"No possibility that he might have been an accomplice?"

"In the robbery?"

"Yes, of course," said DeKok testily. "It wouldn't be the first time."

Vledder waved carelessly.

"We don't know enough . . . yet. It is a fact, however, that the hold-up was very well planned. The Gelder Quay is extremely well suited to cut someone off. The time was also picked with care. It was more or less luck that there was that much money on the truck. Usually it's a lot less."

DeKok pressed his lips together. Then he started to rummage through his pockets and after a short search found a forgotten candy bar. He started to peel off the paper that had stuck to the confection and finally liberated the lumpy chocolate. With a satisfied smile he put the candy in his mouth and dropped the wrappings in a convenient trash can. He chewed thoughtfully.

"I don't believe in coincidences," he said finally. "Especially not when it concerns the robbery of an armored truck." He walked to his desk and sat down. "They found the Alfa Whatever on Dovecote Way?"

Vledder nodded.

"There they transferred to another car. There were impressions of tires on the shoulder and a long streak of rubber on the road. Nothing else."

DeKok glanced at the large clock on the wall. It was exactly thirty-eight minutes past eleven; almost an hour and a half since the robbery. His face, which usually looked like that of a good-natured boxer, now looked more like that of a very depressed bloodhound. He had a feeling that this case was not as simple as it appeared. His instincts had rarely betrayed him in such matters. There was more to it than appeared on the surface and the innocent driver was probably not going to be the only victim of the crime. "Three million," he mused, "in some countries you can have someone killed for just three dollars."

He looked at Vledder, who was preparing the text for an APB.

"You know, Dick," DeKok said sadly, "money . . . money is an invention of the devil. Some are possessed by it."

2

The sky-blue Jaguar raced along the highway.

Richard Sloten relaxed a little. The acute tension that had dulled his thinking, ebbed away. He leaned comfortably back in the seat and lit a cigarette. The sound of the sirens had long since faded away in the distance, resonating in the light fog that hung over Amsterdam and its suburbs. He looked aside and smiled.

"We got out of that just fine. Good getaway. When I first saw those cops near the car, I thought it was the end for us." He smiled again and rubbed his back against the seat. "I'm starting to believe again that we can get away with it." He turned in his seat and cast an affectionate glance at the money bags on the narrow back seat. "How much do you figure?"

Peter pushed his chin out.

"I don't need to figure," he said arrogantly. "I know how much there is."

"How much?"

"Three million."

Richard smirked.

"Three million." He savored the words on his tongue. "Quite a haul. That's one and a half million each."

Peter ignored the remark. He passed a series of trucks at over a hundred miles per hour.

"What time is it?" he asked sharply.

"Quarter to twelve."

Peter nodded to himself.

"Quarter to twelve," he repeated thoughtfully. "It's about time we get off the highway. By now the cops must have found the Alfa Romeo. And it won't take them long to realize we changed to this car. Before you know it, we'll run into a road block." He glanced at Richard and wrinkled his nose at the cigarette smoke. "Where are your gloves?" he asked suddenly.

Richard seemed flustered.

"In my pocket."

"How long have they been there?"

With a shaking hand Richard extinguished his cigarette in the ash tray.

"I . . . eh, I don't know."

Peter snorted contemptuously. His face was getting red and his nostrils quivered.

"Did you take them off in the Alfa?"

Richard shrugged, the tension was coming back.

"Maybe . . . I don't know."

Peter shook his head in disgust.

"How long have you been stealing? Where are your brains? Calls me an idiot! The first thing they do is check the Alfa for prints." He sighed. "I bet they already know that one of the robbers is Richard Sloten."

He glanced aside again, a sharp, observant look for all its brief duration. Then he momentarily blinked his eyes and projected the profile on his retina, as if to burn it into his memory forever more. Yes, he thought, the chin is too weak.

* * *

Vledder replaced the telephone.

"Quick work from the fingerprint experts," he praised, "they found prints all over the Alfa Romeo and matched them with Richard Sloten."

DeKok looked up.

"Do we know him?"

Vledder nodded.

"He just got out. He was here about ten months ago. I think I remember him, about twenty-five, good-looking guy. Well dressed and good manners. His mother used to bring him his meals. Apparently our kitchen wasn't good enough for him."

"Who handled that at the time?"

"Zwakberg."

"What for?"

"Theft. He had stolen an expensive camera from a tourist's car. A couple of constables nailed him, still in the car. They had no proof as to whether or not he also tried to steal the car, but he had the camera in his hands and they charged him with that. Zwakberg was convinced that Sloten wasn't interested in the contents of the car, however."

"Explain."

"As I said. The car itself. That was his specialty. Grand theft auto. Usually expensive models . . . Daimlers, Jaguars, Porsches. He's been convicted several times."

"Is that all?" asked DeKok, for whom one car was much like another.

"What do you mean, isn't it enough?"

"No arrests or convictions for violence?"

"No," said Vledder, shaking his head. "That's not his style. Actually, I don't think there's any violence in him. He never even resisted arrest."

DeKok rubbed the bridge of his nose with a little finger.

"Any partners? Accomplices?"

"Not as far as I know. I'll check it, of course, but as far as I know, he always operated on his own. The only accomplice, if that's what you can call it, is a car dealer near Enschede. An older man. He used to buy the stolen vehicles from Richard, changed engine and chassis numbers and took care of the new paperwork. Then the cars were sold in Belgium and Germany. They worked together for some time until the State Police finally put a stop to it." Vledder shook his head again. "No, Richard Sloten doesn't seem the type to get involved with violence, especially murder."

DeKok rubbed his chin, a thoughtful look on his face.

"Maybe he wasn't even there."

Vledder looked surprised.

"What do you mean?"

"Maybe," explained DeKok, "he wasn't part of the robbery at all."

"And what about his prints?" challenged Vledder.

"His prints could have been left in the car when he stole it."

Vledder grinned, an understanding look on his face.

"Of course. Not a bad idea at all. After all, Sloten's specialty was the *stealing* of cars. So he stole an Alfa Romeo for the actual perpetrators. And that was his sole involvement. I wouldn't be at all surprised if he also stole a second, or maybe even a third escape vehicle for them."

Vledder suddenly stopped talking and made some frantic movements on his keyboard. Then he shuffled through the notes on his desk. Finally back to the computer again.

"What's the matter?" asked DeKok.

"The Jaguar," mumbled Vledder, finally bringing a report up on his screen.

"What Jaguar?"

"Here it is," said Vledder. "On Winken Road in Dovecote. A patrol car reported a Jaguar, presumed stolen. As they started to investigate, a red Alfa Romeo passed by at a high rate of speed."

"And?"

"When they finally located the Alfa Romeo, the Jaguar had disappeared."

* * *

Peter drove the Jaguar at a moderate speed through the center of the old village of Diever in the northern province of Drente. In his rear view mirror he could see the comfortable stack of linen bags, filled with currency. It gave him an exciting feeling of power.

Richard Sloten rubbed his handkerchief over the walnut dashboard and the door sills. He glanced through the windshield as the car made a sharp turn.

"Where are we going?"

Peter evaded the question.

"We're almost there. Just a few more minutes." He waved his right hand in an irritated gesture. "And quit that rubbing. That's a waste of time, anyway. If you don't leave fingerprints, you don't have to wipe them away."

Hastily Richard replaced his handkerchief in his pocket. He felt confused and unsure of himself. He longed for a cigarette, but was afraid to give in to the urge. Slowly a vague fear grew stronger within him. A fear of the cold, calculating man behind the wheel next to him.

Outside the small town, Peter increased the speed. His face was distant and expressionless. The rugged beauty of the landscape escaped him. Drente is known for its wild expanses of heather, dotted with ancient rune stones and megalithic tombstones from before the ice age. The province of Drente and some areas in the extreme east of the Netherlands are practically the only areas that are not below sea-level, or man-made. Once upon a time the hairy mammoth and the sabre-toothed tiger roamed here.

But Peter had no eye for the landscape, much less its history. He only saw the road as he listened to the smooth hum of the tires. A few miles beyond the town of Doldersum he braked suddenly and turned into a sandy path among tall conifers.

Richard looked around with wonder.

"What are we doing here?"

Peter stopped the car and set the hand-brake.

"We're parting company."

* * *

Inspector DeKok leaned back and lifted both legs on top of his desk. His face was somber. He contemplated that the start of the investigation into the robbery had been bad. If this was an omen, a sign of things to come, he thought, there was little to look forward to in the immediate future. He glanced at Vledder who was preparing an addition to the report.

"You know," he began, "I think . . ." He did not complete the sentence but looked at a well-dressed man who had just entered the detective room. The man was in his late fifties and carried a soft-drink crate in one hand. As he progressed toward the middle of the room, conversations stopped. The man placed his crate on the floor and sat down on it.

"Yes," said Vledder, glancing up from his computer.

DeKok held up a restraining hand and pointed toward the center of the room. Vledder peered from around his terminal and closed his file. He sat back and stared at the well-dressed man. Before long everybody in the room was silent, even the suspects who were being interrogated. Telephones were placed on hold.

When he had everybody's attention, the well-dressed man stood up and stepped on top of his crate. In a loud voice he began to harangue the people in the room. He complained about the government, the social measures, the balance of payments, parking regulations and the filth in the canals. It lasted a little less than five minutes. Then he stepped down from his crate, picked it up and, without another glance at any of the occupants of the room, he left.

Vledder stared at DeKok.

"Is that him?" he asked.

"Yes" answered DeKok. "It's been a few years since he's last been here, but his repertoire is still just as encompassing and concise as in the past. It took him less than five minutes."

The room came back to life and soon the constant murmur of voices and the shrill sounding of telephones again prevailed, as if nothing had happened.

"You told me about him," said Vledder, "but I really found it hard to believe. I always thought it was one of those stories you tell to rookies."

"I don't have any stories like that," said DeKok.

"What do you think makes him do it?"

"Who knows. Frustration most probably. We're all frustrated at times and would like to smash something, or break something, or just shout out loud. I'm so mad I could scream, is a common saying. Remember a movie, some time back? The character went around saying 'I'm mad as hell, and I'm not going to take it any more!' Well . . . I think that's his problem."

"You know him?"

"Oh yes, when he first started appearing, about ten, fifteen years ago, we tried to stop him, we even arrested him once. But we let him go. He's a respectable businessman. But sometimes things get too much for him and he comes and blames us. It's

23

easier to let him have his say. He doesn't hurt anybody and it never lasts long."

"Well . . ."

"In a way it's a compliment," added DeKok, "it quite takes me back to the days of 'Uncle Police' and the times that we were still seen as the answer to everybody's problems. Now there's often an animosity between us and the public that is regrettable. The public and, I'm sorry to say, too many cops forget that we are, after all public *servants*."

Vledder had heard DeKok's views before and with a wise nod, he returned to his computer.

"As I was saying," continued DeKok, "before we were interrupted. I think we may already be too late. If the robbers were smart enough to have a second car ready then they probably have already abandoned that as well and are now touring around in a third car. There's a good brain behind it all. The improvisation when they discovered cops next to their getaway car, shows a certain amount of raw courage as well."

Vledder tapped the form that had emerged from his printer.

"What about this APB. You still want me to send it?"

DeKok nodded slowly.

"Of course. The telex must be sent. We have to find that other car, that . . . eh, Jaguar, was it?"

Vledder nodded, knowing full well that DeKok was unable to distinguish a Jaguar from any other kind of car. DeKok had once described the difference in cars by referring to three groups: American cars which were always big, unless it was big and square and then it would be a Roll Royce. All other cars were small cars, according to DeKok. Although he did allow for different colors.

"Too bad," said Vledder, "that I didn't make the connection at once when I read the report. If I had been fast enough, we might have had a chance. Who knows where they've gotten to by now."

"Never mind," soothed DeKok. "These things happen. I think it's pretty clever that you made the connection at all. We're not computers, you know." He smiled, lifted his feet off the desk and walked over to the pegs on the wall. "Come," he said, "Let's go for a walk."

Vledder rose.

"Where to?"

His old mentor did not answer at once. Not until he had placed his ridiculous, little hat on his head, did he say: "To a mother who didn't think our kitchen could feed her son in the style to which he was accustomed."

"Mrs. Sloten."

"Got it in one. You have the address?"

* * *

Vledder parked the police VW in the central square next to Palm Canal. They got out of the car and walked toward Triangle Street. They stopped in front of a picturesque, restored facade and looked up. The intimate character of the houses in the Jordaan was a constant surprise to DeKok.

In almost any other city, the Jordaan would have been classified as a slum. But not in Amsterdam. Loving and careful restoration was constantly in progress. Originally the area was settled by Spanish and Portuguese Jews, escaping the persecution of the Inquisition. Later French Huguenots added their culture to the mixture. Jordaan itself is a Dutch bastardization of the French word "Jardin," meaning "garden." Originally the area must have been very much like a garden, with pleasant cottages and wide open spaces. Over the years, the spaces had been filled with small houses and warehouses. Now the only reminder of a garden was the fact that most streets were named after flowers. The Jordaan can be best compared to a mixture of Delancey Street in New York and Soho in London.

"This it?"

Vledder pulled a piece of paper from his breast pocket and verified the address.

"Yes . . . ninety-seven . . . second floor."

The front door was ajar and DeKok pushed it open. Laboriously he hoisted his two hundred pounds up the narrow, creaking staircase. Vledder followed, light of foot.

They stopped in the corridor and knocked on the door. After some time the door was opened by a large woman in a shiny black kimono with wide sleeves and intricate embroidery. She looked at the Inspectors with a question on her face.

The gray sleuth bowed slightly, lifting his decrepit little hat in the air.

"My name is DeKok," he said politely, "DeKok with kay-oh-kay." He pointed at Vledder. "My colleague, Vledder. We're Police Inspectors, attached to Warmoes Street Station." He paused. "Are you Mrs. Sloten?"

She lifted her chin into the air.

"I am."

DeKok turned his hat in his hands.

"We would like to talk to you . . . concerning your son . . . Richard."

Her eyes narrowed.

"You nabbed him again?"

DeKok shook his head.

"No," he said timidly, "but we're afraid he's been involved in a serious crime."

She snorted contemptuously.

"Afraid . . . afraid. I've been afraid for more than ten years. Ever since that kid left school, it's been one misery after another.

26

And always nice words, he's such a smooth talker. Always the promises... *this* would be the last time." With the door knob still in her hand, she stepped back. "Come in, but don't look at the mess."

DeKok looked around but, as usual in a Dutch house, he could find nothing amiss. The room was closely packed with furniture, whatnots in the corners and shelves and pictures on the walls. Small tables seemed to be everywhere among slender chairs in a rococo-type style. But everything was spotless, dust-free and waxed. The only disorder, if such it could be called, was a half-open magazine on one of the tables. On a sideboard was an expensive silver frame with a large color photograph of a blond young man. Next to the frame stood an expensive doll in a colorful, foreign costume.

DeKok pointed at the photo.

"Is that him?"

Mrs. Sloten nodded and closed the door.

"If he would only be good ... he could be a darling boy. Believe me, at heart he's not bad, not evil at all." She came closer and sighed elaborately. "But he takes after my ex-husband ... he likes the good things in life ... luxury. Everything has to be expensive ... his clothes, his cars ... his women. The best is barely good enough."

DeKok took the photo in his hand and studied the portrait intently. Vledder was right; Richard Sloten was a good-looking young man. Regular features, clear blue eyes, a high forehead and dark blond hair. He replaced the photo and turned toward the woman.

"This morning an armed robbery was committed on Gelder Quay. The truck, an armored truck, was run off the road and cut off near New Market. Two men jumped out of an expensive foreign car ..."

"An Alfa Romeo," added Vledder.

27

". . . and forced the personnel out of the truck," continued DeKok blithely. "They were forced to open the back door and remove the money. Then the robbers shot the driver."

Mrs. Sloten brought a hand up to her throat. A flush spread over her face.

"Dead?"

DeKok nodded slowly.

"A father of three children."

She sank down on one of the chairs. She was pale.

"Richard didn't do that," she said evenly. "Not Richard. He doesn't own a weapon. It must have been someone else."

DeKok stared at her.

"Who else?"

Mrs. Sloten did not answer. She seemed to have shrunk, her head was down and her shoulders shook.

DeKok kneeled next to her.

"Who else?" he asked insistently.

She shook her head and sobbed openly.

"Oh, God . . . My God." She lifted a teary face toward him. "You can't ask me to betray my own child."

3

They drove back toward Warmoes Street. Vledder, at the wheel of the decrepit VW Beetle, looked angry.

"No luck," he said.

DeKok looked sad.

"It's too bad," he said. "If Mrs. Sloten had been willing to name Richard's accomplice, we would have been a lot further."

Vledder made an annoyed gesture.

"I don't understand her. If she is willing to admit, in so many words, that her son was connected with the robbery . . . if she is also convinced that her son was not responsible for the killing . . . why won't she just tell us what she knows?"

DeKok pushed his little hat deeper over his eyes.

"The loot," he said calmly.

Vledder reacted sharply.

"The loot. What good is money when you're in jail?"

"Our current judges," shrugged DeKok, "are extremely understanding people. I mean . . . if Richard Sloten can prove that he did not shoot . . . that he was against it completely . . . what do you think he'll get for the robbery? Eighteen months . . . two years?" He glanced aside. "This is not the States where an accomplice to a murder is tried as the murderer himself. So, even if he goes to jail, where can you make at least a million and a half, tax-free, in less than two years?"

"You have to be kidding. Surely the money will be confiscated?"

"Only if it can be found."

"So you think that Mrs. Sloten kept her mouth shut to enable her son to hide his share of the robbery?"

"Possibly. We have no idea what sort of agreements have been made. Perhaps the accomplice will take care of hiding the loot and in a few days we will see Richard, no doubt accompanied by his mother, appear at the station to turn himself in."

"What!?"

"Sure. He'll be full of regret, full of assurances that he didn't mean it that way, never was part of the plan and so on. His mother will confirm that . . . poor Richard just had a hankering for expensive things."

Vledder grinned.

"But then they *will* have to name the accomplice."

DeKok looked surprised.

"But why? We have no way to force Richard to reveal that information, no legal way, I mean. And he will certainly *not* volunteer the information. Even if he wanted to, his lawyer will prevent that, I'm sure. If he reveals his accomplice, he'll endanger the loot . . . and the attorney's fees." He paused. "Besides . . . Richard's continued silence is a mighty weapon to hold over his accomplice's head, to remind him that he has a right to his share. Perhaps more."

Vledder started.

"More?"

"To be sure," nodded DeKok. "Keep in mind that when Richard has completed his sentence, the other man will still be wanted for armed robbery . . . for murder. There's no statute of limitations on murder and who will be the most important witness when we catch him?"

"Richard Sloten."

"Exactly. And that way Richard has an excellent weapon to blackmail his former accomplice." He pushed his lower lip forward. "Believe me, if that's the way the game is to be played, we're a long way from a solution . . ." He stopped suddenly and pointed at a waving man. "There's Jan Graaf."

Vledder steered toward the curb and stopped in front of the man. DeKok opened the window.

"What's up, Jan?"

Inspector Graaf leaned forward, his bearded face filled the opening in the door.

"Are you heading back to the station?" He glanced at the communication gear in the car. "Oh, I see, radio switched off again, eh? Well, there's a girl waiting for you."

"What sort of girl?"

"A beauty . . . a princess . . . a picture. Seldom, no, never, seen as good-looking a woman before. I asked her if I could help her, but she wanted to talk only to you."

"What about?"

Jan Graaf grimaced and pulled his beard.

"Women's rights for all I know. I didn't ask." He closed both eyes momentarily. "But she is certainly worth seeing."

DeKok smiled.

"Well, if you say so . . ." He closed the window and motioned toward Vledder. With a last wave at Graaf, the car pulled away from the curb and shortly thereafter Vledder parked in front of the station house.

* * *

31

She walked in front of them with short, decisive steps. Her hips swayed pleasantly and the long, blonde hair danced on her shoulders. DeKok sniffed. The mild scent of her perfume had a sensual effect. In the small interrogation room he pointed at a chair and watched her sit down. Graaf had been right, he reflected. He had never seen a more beautiful woman. Although in his long career and because of his proximity to the Red Light District he had been in contact with many beautiful women, this one was special. He was reminded of a movie star from the past, Merle Oberon, or something like that. The reason he remembered was because she had married a Dutchman. He sat down across from her and looked at her with pleasure. It would be easy, he thought, to become totally enraptured by the woman. He glanced at Vledder who stared at her with open admiration in his eyes. She was small, but perfectly proportioned and her ivory skin was without a blemish, or the least trace of make-up, apart from a hint of lipstick. Perfect legs and slender arms. Well manicured, smooth hands. The body of a goddess, he thought, until he looked at the bright, almond shaped eyes glistening with an exotic light. Then he realized that the eyes were cold, without feeling. Inside this perfect figure was a cool, calculating mind. He shivered inwardly. He had looked into the eyes of a snake, or totally self-absorbed evil.

The impression was as real as it was fleeting. She blinked her long lashes and when he looked again, the eyes looked like he had expected them to look, more in keeping with the beautiful, graceful appearance of his visitor. But he could not rid himself of that brief, revealing sight he had seen for just a moment. With that, his police persona re-established itself.

"You asked for me?" he asked pleasantly.

She nodded, apparently unsure of herself.

"You're Inspector DeKok?"

"Yes, with kay-oh-kay," he said automatically.

She laughed, relaxed. A vivacious sound, like that of tinkling crystal.

"My name is Monika . . . Monika Buwalda." She laughed again with that cheerful, tinkling sound. "I have been told you are in charge of the case."

"What case?"

"The armed robbery this morning. Now that one of the drivers was killed, they said, it would certainly be assigned to DeKok."

"Who are *they*?"

She made a vague gesture with an elegant hand.

"Friends . . . I would rather not name names."

DeKok pursed his lips.

"Well," he said, "your friends are well informed."

Monika ignored the remark.

"It was quite a surprise to me. I would never have thought Richard capable of such a deed."

DeKok feigned ignorance.

"What deed?"

"The robbery. Richard was involved."

"Which Richard?"

"Richard Sloten."

DeKok gave her a sharp look.

"How do you know?"

Monika Buwalda made a nervous gesture. Despite himself, DeKok had to suppress the urge to take her in his arms and soothe her. He looked at her eyes and easily suppressed the urge. Monika was unaware that she had lost a conquest.

"He told me so himself," she said in a voice that went well with the tinkling laugh he had heard before. The voice was clear and innocent, but with a sexy, seductive quality designed to bring any man under its spell. "We have discussed it for some time," she continued. "Richard felt it was his one chance to get rich forever."

DeKok bit his lower lip.

"Why was Richard so forthcoming? I mean why would he discuss a crime with you?"

A dangerous flame lit up, deep in the brown eyes.

"Why me?" she asked indignantly. "After all, I *am* his fiancee."

DeKok looked surprised.

"You're engaged to Richard?" he asked, disbelief in his voice, "officially engaged to be married?"

Monika shook her head with irritation. The beauty of her face was not marred, despite the slight frown on her forehead.

"I mean, what's engaged? That's a bit old-fashioned, of course." It sounded casual. "Richard and I live together and we like the fast life. Intense and fast. We haven't got a second to waste. It's a race with time. We must enjoy now . . . now, while we're still young."

DeKok nodded his understanding.

"And for that money is a prerequisite."

She lowered her eyes in a demure gesture that no longer was able to fool DeKok.

"A lot of money," she agreed. She looked at him and pushed a strand of hair behind one ear with an enticing gesture. Everything she did seemed calculated to arouse passion in a man. "Yes, a lot of money," she went on, "if you want to do it right, the way we want to do it. Live life . . . totally . . . without restrictions."

"No matter what?"

She gave him a hard look and for a moment he was again struck by the cold reptilian expression in her eyes.

"If necessary," she said.

DeKok rubbed his chin.

"And that's an excuse?"

"Excuse for what?"

"For killing a man."

Monika sighed. Her bosom heaved and she crossed her legs. She stroked her forehead and for a moment DeKok expected her to faint elegantly. Despite her extreme beauty, every gesture started to look theatrical, especially after having looked into her eyes.

"That's why I came," she said softly, almost whispering. "I came because I did not want the death of that poor man." She looked up and added, suddenly, vehemently: "And neither did Richard." She sighed again, seemed to collapse but then gave the impression of holding on to reality with extreme effort.

Vledder glanced at DcKok who remained unaffected. Vledder himself obviously was deeply influenced by Monika's beauty and did not see any of her gestures as theatrical. He was a bit annoyed with DeKok for his unfeeling, official attitude toward the beautiful woman.

"Well?" prompted DeKok.

"We wanted money," she confessed. "A lot of money to enable us to live as we want."

DeKok closed his eyes. His calvinistic upbringing rebelled at the thinly disguised, limitless egoism that came through in her statements. He suppressed his anger and continued the interview.

"Richard Sloten," he said, "was the accomplice in an armed robbery and in a murder. This is prohibited by Law. Our society simply does not condone that type of behavior . . . no matter what the motivation. I can assure you that we will do everything possible to arrest him."

Monika looked frightened.

"Richard? But why Richard? Richard never killed anybody. It was that addict, that damned junkie and his gun."

* * *

Vledder frowned.

"Peter Shot?"

"I've never heard of him before, either," admitted DeKok. "What do you have on him?"

Vledder consulted his computer.

"Just what Monika told us," he said. "An American addict of Dutch origin, from Houston, Texas. Apparently he's wanted by the police there for a series of armed robberies. He may have killed an American cop as well." He snorted. "That was supposedly Richard's accomplice . . . a cop killer."

DeKok nodded thoughtfully.

"I'm surprised he managed to leave the States. Our American colleagues are most efficient and certainly so when one of their own has been killed."

"Yes," said Vledder, "for a cop killer they've been known to ignore jurisdictions. Everybody is on the look-out for him. Good thing, too."

"Why do you say that? A killer is a killer."

"Yes, but somebody who kills a cop, is doubly dangerous. It's the type of person that will fight it out with an armed opponent and is more likely to kill at random. He, or she, also shows a marked disrespect for authority, for the Laws that are intended to protect all of us."

"There's something in what you say. Be that as it may, however, Monika Buwalda is convinced that he's the man who killed the driver. Apparently she doesn't think her own Richard is capable of murder."

Vledder grimaced.

"And what does that mean in real terms?"

"Nothing," admitted DeKok readily. "Not much, anyway. But it does coincide with what Mrs. Sloten said about her son. There seems to be some agreement on Richard's character."

"What about the name," asked Vledder, "you think it's his real name . . . Peter Shot?"

DeKok shook his head.

"It's a nickname. Probably has something to do with his addiction. I guess he has a shot every time before committing a crime, or something like that."

"That doesn't help us much. There's nobody by that name in my system. What about Monika? How well do you think she knew him?"

DeKok spread his hands in a gesture of surrender.

"You heard. She met him a few times. Richard introduced him to her. But during those meetings they never discussed the robbery. Peter spoke excellent Dutch, almost without an accent."

Vledder scratched the back of his neck.

"As I said, I've never heard of him." He shook his head. "But then . . . Amsterdam is beginning to resemble a gathering place for international criminals. Before you know it, we'll be like Chicago in the thirties."

"Not so somber," laughed DeKok. He stood up and started to pace up and down the room. His eyes stared into the distance as he avoided obstacles with subconscious ease. After a while he stopped in front of the window and stared out over the rooftops of the District, softly rocking on the balls of his feet. Then he turned toward Vledder.

"We have to establish Peter Shot's real identity as soon as possible," he said. "If we can enlist Monika's cooperation, that shouldn't be too difficult. At least she can identify him." He raised a finger in the air. "Why don't you have Interpol check it out with the Houston Police. Perhaps they know a bit more about our elusive Peter. They may have his fingerprints, or a mug shot."

Vledder made a note on his pad as his other hand went for the telephone. Then he hesitated.

"How long do you think Peter has been in Holland?"

DeKok shrugged.

"That's anybody's guess. We should probably have a talk with our colleagues in Narcotics. As an addict he might be known to them. Perhaps they have encountered him somewhere."

"What about his possible residence?"

"Really, Dick," said DeKok impatiently. "Who knows. According to Monika she met him once at her house, once in the street and once in an abandoned building."

"You think Peter lived in the abandoned building ... squatted there?"

"It's a possibility. I'm sure that Peter was reluctant to have himself registered under his own name. After all, we have an extradition treaty with the United States and if they wanted him for killing a cop, he would be on the next plane out. No, Peter would have been very cautious about his true identity."

"So, how did he get here?"

"That's not all that difficult anymore, these days. As I understand it, it's relatively easy for an American to go to Mexico. From there to any of the countries of the EEC and he's home free. Nobody checks papers anymore, once you're in Europe."

"Uhu," grunted Vledder, "and now that he has a lot of money, it will be that much easier for him."

The telephone on DeKok's desk rang. Vledder stretched out and lifted the receiver. He listened intently and then told the caller to hold.

"What is it?" asked DeKok.

"They found Richard Sloten."

"And?"

"Killed."

DeKok swallowed.

"Finish the call," he said.

4

Inspector DeKok looked somberly into the distance. The lines around his mouth were frozen into a serious expression. The news of Richard's death had touched him more than he had expected. The feeling bothered him, he could not place it, could not discover why this should be so. As far as he knew he had never met the young man in his life. Yet, a feeling of pity burned in his heart. Slowly he turned toward Vledder.

"Where did they find him?"

The young Inspector was still pale.

"On a sandy path in the woods around Doldersum."

"Doldersum? Where is that?"

"The western part of Drente. The path connects to the road to Doldersum. It's a beautiful area. I've been on vacation there, several times. Apparently a man, well-known to the local cops as an incorrigible poacher, found him. He immediately alerted the police." DeKok nodded to himself, while Vledder continued: "Two neck shots . . . from close by."

"Just like the driver."

Vledder nodded slowly, his hands busy on the keyboard of his terminal.

"Obviously Richard Sloten was killed by his partner in crime. There were some tire tracks. The local cops will preserve them. But it seems they may match the Jaguar."

DeKok rubbed his chin.

"From close up," he murmured. "In the neck." He shivered visibly. "Like an execution."

He leaned forward in his chair and rested his head on his folded hands, elbows on the desk. His thoughts drifted away. In his mind's eye he went over every known detail of the two murders, searching to get a grip on the character, the identity of the killer. But the picture remained vague. A faint smile played around his lips.

"He won't have to divide by three, anymore," he said with a sigh.

Vledder looked up from his terminal.

"By three . . . who is the third one?"

DeKok grinned mirthlessly.

"The tipster, the man who told Richard that the transport contained an extraordinary amount of money."

"The driver?"

DeKok shrugged.

"It could . . ." There was hesitation in his voice. "It could have been the reason he was killed. When we take that into consideration, the killing of the driver wasn't all that senseless. I'm beginning to think that Peter Shot knew exactly what he was doing as he systematically wiped out those with whom he might have had to share the loot."

Vledder shook his head.

"That certainly gives us some indication of a sinister brain."

DeKok nodded.

"Some are that way."

He stood up, a more cheerful look on his face.

"It's about time," said DeKok.

"For what?" asked Vledder.

DeKok laughed, banishing the murderer to the back of his mind.

"For Lowee . . . and a cognac."

* * *

Lowee, because of his diminutive size, generally referred to as "Little Lowee," hastily wiped his hands on his vest as he greeted DeKok jovially.

"Well come . . . well come," he chirped. "I been wondering if crime done locked you up in the station house forever. As a matter of fac' I was wondering iffen I shoudna have hired a coupla wise guys to help break you out."

DeKok laughed heartily, as always refreshed by Lowee's undisguised delight in seeing him and in Lowee's version of Dutch. The small barkeeper spoke invariably in Amsterdam thieves' language which will cause even born Amsterdammers to think twice before they grasp the meaning.

"Lowee," said DeKok with feeling, "your concern is a balm for my heart." He moved toward the end of the bar and hoisted himself onto his favorite stool, his back against the wall. Vledder sat down next to him. More and more Vledder was becoming reconciled to these frequent visits to Lowee's establishment.

However, the small barkeeper continued to regard the young Inspector with a certain amount of suspicion. After all, Vledder was a cop, but DeKok was a friend. Vledder was still too rigid, too concerned with rules and regulations, too much concerned with his own importance and dignity as a cop. DeKok was different. DeKok was part of the Quarter. The fact that DeKok once, in the dim past, had been instrumental in Lowee's incarceration for several years, had nothing to do with the genuine friendship between the small barkeeper and the gray sleuth. In some way it seemed to have tightened the bonds of friendship between the two. Police was a necessary evil, philosophized Lowee. Without cops it would really be a mess and what would be the fun of being bad, if nobody enforced what was right?

Now he looked up at DeKok, a broad smile on his friendly, mousy face.

"Same recipe?"

Without waiting for an answer, the barkeeper dived under the counter and produced a venerable bottle of cognac. With almost the same gesture he produced three large snifters and after allowing DeKok a few seconds to admire the label, Lowee poured generous measures in the glasses.

DeKok looked on with an approving smile on his face. He loved these moments. He lifted his glass and slowly rocked it in the cradle of his hand. Then he leaned forward and sniffed the aroma. A look of pure delight transformed his face as he took his first, careful sip.

He replaced the glass on the counter and leaned closer.

"You read the paper yet?"

Little Lowee glanced at him from aside.

"You means the job on the money truck?"

DeKok laughed.

"You're especially sharp today."

The barkeeper sniffed in contempt.

"Takes no genie brain to figure it out. I just smells it's your case."

DeKok looked serious.

"They killed one of the men on the truck," he said sadly. "Just like that. I mean, there was no reason."

Lowee wiped the counter absent-mindedly.

"I done read that."

DeKok gave him a penetrating look.

"You know anything about it?"

"You mean, diddi knows it's gonna happen?"

"Exactly."

The barkeeper shook his head.

"Nah, it was a surprise for me too, you knows."

DeKok took another sip.

"So, none of the regulars were involved?"

Lowee grimaced.

"As I said . . . 'eard nuthin' about it. And I hears somethin', now and again, you knows. Them guys *drink* here, after all."

DeKok nodded his understanding.

"Ever hear of a Peter Shot?"

The barkeeper did not answer at once. His eyes narrowed as he contemplated his friend.

"Peter Shot?"

"Yes."

"A junkie?"

DeKok gestured vaguely.

"That's what's being said. He likes to take a shot regularly, especially just before a job. It may account for his nickname."

The friendly face of the small barkeeper became hard. He pressed his lips together in a disapproving grimace. Finally he exploded.

"A rat," he said out loud. "Yessir, a rat, and I'm sorry to insult all them rats that is rats. He's a gangster, pure and simple. An American import, you knows. One of them that got no other place to go and now comes 'ere to play Al Capone in Mokum.* Iffen we don't get tougher with them criminals, we is gonna get more and more of them. An honest burglar can 'ardly make a living no more." He shook his head sadly.

Mokum: Amsterdam slang for "Amsterdam." The origin of the word is lost, but it is always used affectionately like *The Big Apple* for New York.

DeKok laughed.

"Apparently you know him."

The barkeeper snorted contemptuously and drained his glass with one big swallow.

"He done been here just oncet . . . a coupla months ago. I kicked 'im out, tha's what I did. I hate them macho punks that wave them heaters around for no good reason at all."

"Is that what he did?"

Lowee was getting more excited.

"He done sit here at the bar, abraggin' and lying about all the big jobs 'e done in the States. One of the guys sorta says he were lying and that nut pulls out a heater. I done killed a cop, 'e says, so what stops me from killin' you?"

"Then you kicked him out?"

Lowee nodded vehemently.

"I done tole him I was gonna call the cops. Somehow that scared him and he split. I never done seen 'im again."

"You know where he lives?"

"Nah, notta clue. You wants him?"

"Yes."

"For the truck job?"

DeKok nodded slowly.

"I have reason to believe that he and Richard Sloten committed that crime."

Little Lowee smiled.

"Slick Ricky . . . notta chance. Not 'is style at all."

DeKok sighed.

"No . . . it was his death."

Lowee looked tense.

"His death?" he asked breathlessly.

"Yes," nodded DeKok. "His partner put two bullets in his neck."

The barkeeper swallowed nervously. A tic developed on his narrow cheeks.

"The rat," he hissed. "I *tole* you he were a rat!"

DeKok nodded resignedly.

"That you did," he admitted. "Come, pour one for the road."

* * *

From Lowee's bar they walked towards New Market and from there, through Emperors Street toward Crooked Tree Ditch. DeKok looked around. There was not a tree in sight. But the name did not come from the trees along the canal, but from the use of the canal in times past. It was one of the channels used to float trees toward the busy shipyards in the 17th and 18th Century. There was Straight Tree Ditch and Crooked Tree Ditch, the latter having a distinct bend in the middle. The trees had been removed to allow easier access to the work pits of the Metro under construction. All over Amsterdam such unsightly scenes were being repeated. Because of the wet ground and the fact that Amsterdam is below sea level, a different kind of construction was required in many places. Complete segments of tunnel were being built above ground and then literally sunk into the mud, down to the required depth. These sections were then connected to other, similar sections, or to sections built in the more conventional way by means of tunneling. The City Fathers had promised that the temporary devastation of the city-scape would be restored to its original splendor, once the work was done. And indeed, there were additional plans to restore canals in the streets that once had them filled in to accommodate the ever growing increase of traffic.

DeKok thoroughly approved. He regretted the uprooting of age old building and the trees that could never be replaced the way they were. But the restoration of former canals was an appropriate compensation for the temporary blight.

Near the bridge leading to King Street, DeKok stood still and looked at a dilapidated facade. Vledder looked up as well.

"Do we have business here?" asked Vledder.

"Yes, here we'll find Carmen Manouskicheck."

"Carmen Manu . . . what?"

"Manouskicheck . . . an old friend." There was warmth in his voice when he continued. "She came here after the Hungarian revolution, dabbled in prostitution for a while and then became an addict. Now she's a small dealer."

"Cocaine? Heroin? Crack?"

"Heroin. She sells to the people who don't want to frequent the more usual places and who want to avoid the attention of the police."

Vledder approached the flaked, almost paintless, door.

"We have to go in here?"

DeKok restrained him.

"Wait just a moment."

"Why?"

"Give her time to hide her stash."

"Whatever for?" Vledder was nonplussed and belligerent.

DeKok pointed at a number of strategically placed mirrors, like the rear view mirrors of cars, enabling the occupant to see the entire stretch of street, without sticking a head out of the window.

"You see," he explained. "She's already seen us. If we hurry her, she'll flush the stuff down the toilet."

Vledder shrugged off DeKok's gentle restraint and looked impatient.

"So what."

DeKok rubbed the corners of his eyes with a tired gesture.

"Then tonight," he said slowly, reluctantly, "she'll have to drag her tired, sick body out into the streets to make enough money to replace her needs. I'd like to spare her that, if I can."

Vledder growled.

"Then she shouldn't use the junk."

DeKok did not react. He looked up again and then slowly, deliberately walked toward the weathered door. Wearily he climbed the steep staircase. Vledder followed, still moody.

Carmen Manouskicheck waited for them at the top of the stairs, leaning against the peeling, grimy door opening to her room. There was a slight smile around her sunken mouth and the beginning of a happy light in the hollow eyes.

"DeKok . . . DeKok in person." It sounded mocking and gay at the same time. "That I should live so long," she continued, sticking out her left arm and showing the inside, marked by needle tracks and infected scabs. "Want to see if I killed myself yet?"

The gray cop looked at her for several seconds. His glance searched the lines in her face. He clearly saw the signs of decay, of impending death. Another year, at most, he said to himself. Then she would be one more over-dosed corpse.

"Hello Carmen, my girl."

His voice was warm and sympathetic, without a trace of the dismay he felt at seeing her deterioration.

Suddenly she lost her poise. She lowered her head and the long, lusterless hair veiled her face. When she looked up again there were tears in her eyes.

"Come in," she said softly and turned back into the room.

The two Inspectors followed her.

Vledder looked around. The small room was sparsely furnished. There was a table with four wooden chairs. An old chest, one of the legs replaced by a few bricks to keep it level, leaned against one wall. On the floor, in a corner was a mattress

49

with some sheets and an old blanket that served as bed. Worn linoleum covered the floor. Except for the unmade bed, everything was painfully clean, but the dismal surroundings and the old furniture made the room look shabby and grimy.

Carmen pulled two bolts to bar the door. Then she gestured toward the bare table.

"Have a seat." She seemed to have recovered somewhat and dried her tears with her sleeve. "Or are you here with a search warrant."

DeKok shook his head.

"I came because of Peter Shot."

She gave him a suspicious look.

"What do you want with him?"

DeKok smiled.

"At least you know him."

Carmen nodded slowly.

"I know him, yes. He came here once in a while ... shopping."

DeKok looked at her evenly.

"Came?"

Her expression changed. A little color returned to the tawny, dried out cheeks.

"He doesn't show anymore. It's been weeks. And he still owes me money."

"You know where he lives?"

She shook her head.

"Here, there and everywhere. But he isn't here and also nowhere else. I asked everybody. It seems Peter Shot has disappeared from sight."

5

Vledder aimed the old VW at the Berlage Bridge. Across the bridge he turned left toward the Amstel Dike. He navigated through the busy Amsterdam traffic with the elan of a cabbie and the ease of an experienced race driver.

DeKok was silent. He was seated, as usual, next to Vledder in the passenger seat, his body swaying gently in the seat belts. He was thinking about the hints and clues they had gathered so far. There was not much to go on. Two men had robbed an armored truck in broad daylight. Three million was stolen and one of the drivers had been purposely killed. One of the perpetrators, Richard Sloten, had been found dead a few hours later in the far-off province of Drente. And the remaining perpetrator? As far as they had been able to determine, Peter Shot, had disappeared without a trace long before the robbery. A strange case, to say the least. DeKok rubbed his eyes and sighed.

What about the three million? He looked up. They were driving along the Amstel river, the river that had given Amsterdam its name. The left bank of the river was hidden by houseboats, that completely blocked the view of the water. The area was messy, dilapidated, with the wrecks of automobiles scattered here and there. DeKok shook his head. With one hand the city council had promised that the Metro would have no impact on the scenic beauty of his beloved city and then on the other hand, that same city council totally neglected different aspects of the same environment they had sworn to protect.

He pushed himself higher in the seat.

"What time is the funeral?"

"Eleven."

"You received a notification?"

"No."

"Did you speak to Mrs. Muller?"

Vledder shook his head.

"I have not seen her at all."

"Why not?"

Vledder's face fell.

"Yesterday, after the official autopsy, I turned the corpse over to the funeral home. The guy from the funeral home said that Mrs. Muller was still so overcome by grief, that it was almost impossible to talk to her. She cries almost constantly and is under doctor's care. There's apparently no family to support her."

DeKok nodded to himself.

"Who took care of the funeral arrangements?"

"Mr. Houten."

"Who?"

"A charming, very suave man," smiled Vledder. "Director of the firm where Martin Muller worked. He arranged everything and paid for everything and he assured me that he would support Mrs. Muller financially for as long as was necessary."

DeKok rubbed the bridge of his nose with a little finger.

"How noble," he said. "Did you happen to discuss the robbery with him?"

"No, I didn't think it wise at the time. I'd rather leave that to you. I just called him on the phone, you see . . . about the funeral. That's all."

"So, you did not meet him personally?"

"No."

DeKok gave him a surprised look.

"But you decided he was charming and suave?"

Vledder seemed irritated.

"Well, that's the impression he gave over the phone."

"Careful, Dick," chided DeKok, "don't let your instincts run away with you."

* * *

There was not a lot of interest. There were just a few cars parked near the entrance to Sorrow Field. A Renault, an Opel, a Datsun. A rusty "Ugly Duckling," Citroen's grand experiment, was parked between a Rolls Royce and a late-model Porsche. Vledder identified the cars as they passed and DeKok, totally disinterested, merely grunted.

They parked close to the entrance and walked along the gravel path to the Chapel. It drizzled and DeKok pulled up the collar of his raincoat and pushed his little hat further down on his forehead.

A number of people, with somber faces, were waiting outside the Chapel. The doors opened and they entered. DeKok took off his hat and found a place near the back of the room. Vledder stood next to him. Solemn organ sounds descended from above and when the last notes had died away, a graying man in a black robe walked toward the pulpit. He coughed impressively and talked about Satan, who apparently ruled the world now that people, bedazzled by luxury, had lost the way to God.

At first DeKok listened intently, fascinated by the unctuous voice of the speaker, but soon the oily voice stripped the meaning of the very words that were uttered. They passed by without touching him, or the audience. DeKok's eyes roamed over the mourners.

Near the front was a young woman, dressed in black. Her hair was a striking blonde. Despite the hat and the dark veil that covered her face, the golden color of the hair sparkled brightly in the diffused light of the Chapel. To her right was a small boy, earnest, with a pale face. DeKok figured him to be about seven, or eight, years old. To her left were two girls, small and pleasingly plump and with the same striking, blonde hair. Their legs moved rhythmically, restlessly, from the edge of the seat. They were obviously bored and having to sit still, for so long, was a torture to them.

Just behind the young woman were a number of men, ill at ease in their best suits. They were big and rough looking. DeKok pegged them as colleagues of the murdered driver. Slightly apart were two gentlemen in trendy, fashionable, exquisitely cut clothes. DeKok's gaze rested on them for a while. He pulled his lower lip and wondered who belonged to the fast car he had seen outside. The model reminded him of the cars used by the Dutch Highway Patrol. He had long since forgotten, as an unimportant detail, that the car was a Porsche.

Again the organ music descended from the ceiling. The man in the black robe had disappeared. Professional pallbearers arranged themselves around the coffin. In keeping with the efficient Dutch way of funerals, the doors behind the coffin opened. Gray daylight streamed in and the mourners prepared to follow the coffin. A new group of mourners, DeKok knew, was already gathering in front of the entrance to the non-denominational Chapel for the next funeral.

The pallbearers lifted the coffin and proceeded outside into the drizzle. The mourners followed, Vledder and DeKok bringing up the rear.

Vledder wiped the rain from his face. He did not like cemeteries, or funerals.

"Why are we here anyway?" he asked moodily.

DeKok did not turn toward him, but kept his eyes on the procession in front.

"We're here to render last honors to a man who had become too dangerous to stay alive."

Vledder smiled grimly.

"Dead men carry no tales."

DeKok nodded agreement.

"But yet . . . I would have liked to have known what he *could* have said."

Vledder gave him an incredulous look.

"And that's why we're here?"

DeKok pointed at the mourners.

"Martin Muller was undeniably involved in the robbery. The question remains: how? Was he an accomplice . . . a dangerous witness, or merely a victim?"

Vledder dug his hands deep in his pockets. His face was serious.

"Then there must also be some sort of connection between Martin and Peter Shot."

DeKok did not react at once. A new idea had formed. Suddenly he saw a possible connection which had not been considered before.

"Perhaps," he said, hesitating, "perhaps . . . Martin was killed on orders from somebody."

Vledder was surprised.

"Who?"

DeKok glanced at his partner.

"On the orders of whomever wanted him dead."

The procession stopped near the open grave site. With routine movements the pallbearers lowered the coffin and placed it on the lift. They removed the black cloth covering, folded it and stepped back. The rain could be heard clearly in the sudden silence as it ticked on the lid of the coffin. The young woman cried soundlessly, leaning for support on the shoulder of the small boy next to her. One of the well-dressed gentlemen stepped forward and announced that, at the request of the family, there would be no speeches. He stepped back within the circle.

At a gesture from DeKok, Vledder stepped forward quickly and examined the seal that closed off the last resting place of a murder victim. He nodded at DeKok, indicating the seals were still intact and stepped back. At a silent signal from one of the pallbearers, a slight whirring indicated the lift engaging and slowly the coffin sank from view.

DeKok observed the mourners. The well-dressed gentlemen were young, perhaps in their early thirties. One of the heavy truck drivers was a man who, years ago, had been arrested for burglary. He tried to remember the name, but his memory failed him. Next to DeKok a handsome, athletically built man murmured softly. DeKok strained his ears.

"So long, Martin," said the man.

DeKok stepped back and walked away from the grave. Vledder, who had unobtrusively circled the group, joined him a little later. From a distance they watched the group as it moved away from the grave.

Vledder looked at his partner.

"Well," he said, vexation in his voice, "can we get out of the rain now? All these gravestones give me the creeps."

DeKok nodded vaguely, his mind on other things.

By a round-about route they reached the gate. Their old, decrepit VW Beetle was the only car left, apart from a large number of limousines that had not been there before. Apparently the next funeral was a more expensive affair.

Suddenly Vledder started to run. DeKok called after him, surprise on his face.

"What's got into you?"

Vledder turned, but did not slacken his pace.

"There's a guy in our car."

* * *

DeKok recognized the man who had said 'So long, Martin,' at the grave site. He gave him a searching look.

"The car wasn't locked?"

The man shook his head.

"It was raining, I felt the door handle and it was open, so I crawled inside to wait. You see, I want to talk to you." He cocked his head. "After all, you're the police, aren't you?"

The gray sleuth nodded.

"DeKok, with, eh, with kay-oh-kay." He pointed a thumb at Vledder. "My colleague, Inspector Vledder."

The man sighed elaborately.

"Peter . . . Peter Doon. Usually I'm not all that presumptuous. That isn't me at all. I'm not in the habit of getting into other people's cars. But then, this is almost a public vehicle, isn't it. I don't like to get in contact with the police, either. Not to put too fine a point on it: you're not exactly my favorite kind of people. But Martin was my mate. He and I have been on the international routes together, mostly to Czecho-Slovakia, when that was still one country . . . glass and pottery. Other countries, too, mostly in the Balkans. I thought it was a real shame when he left the long trips for the armored cars."

"And when did that happen?"

"A few months ago."

"Why?"

Doon moved uneasily on the narrow back seat.

57

"Ria ... Martin's wife ... is a good-looking woman. You've seen her. Class, so to speak and really worth looking at." He paused. "When you're on the long trips, you're away from home a lot ... never less than a week. Nothing you can do about that, it's the nature of the business. But with money transports you're home every night, you see."

DeKok nodded.

"And he didn't trust Ria."

Peter Doon looked thoughtful.

"Well, I wouldn't exactly say that. He loved her. He'd die for her, literally. But there was talk, on the job ... and in his neighborhood."

"What sort of talk?"

The man scratched behind his ear.

"Ria ... Ria was supposed to be having an affair."

"With whom?"

Peter Doon hesitated again. He was obviously in a quandary. But loyalty to his dead mate loosened his tongue eventually.

"Mr. Houten."

DeKok gave him a sharp look.

"One of the Directors?"

Doon nodded soberly.

"That's what they said." He placed a hand on his barrel chest. "You must understand," he added, "I don't know if it's true. People say so many things. But Martin was behaving a bit strangely, lately. That's why I can't understand why he deviated from his route."

DeKok swallowed.

"What?"

Peter Doon nodded calmly.

"He should never have been on Gelder Quay with his truck."

6

"Any news from Houston?"

Vledder nodded.

"I by-passed Interpol . . . too slow. I contacted the Houston police direct. Much to my surprise I got a Detective-Sergeant Hollander on the line. He was just as surprised when he suddenly received a call from a Dutch cop. But as usual, our American colleagues were immediately ready to help any way they could. He promised to call me back within the hour."

"And?"

Vledder shook his head.

"Nothing. It seems that the nickname 'Shot' isn't all that unusual over there . . . in a number of connections. There's no way to figure that out. The Houston police was ready to give me thousands of names. Even the fact that Peter was supposed to have shot a cop, wasn't much of a clue. Sadly, about five hundred cops are shot in the line of duty over there, every year. And robberies are a dime a dozen."

"So, not a chance?"

Vledder shrugged carelessly.

"No, the Houston police will do what they can, but without fingerprints they don't expect much result."

DeKok grinned.

"I'm glad I don't have their problems," he said. "We've only about fifteen million to worry about and if we accept that at least 10% of the population is involved in some sort of criminal activity, we've still only to worry about less than two million. But in the States that number must be at least twenty-five million, or more. They certainly have a lot more murders over there, but five hundred cops a year . . . it seems inconceivable. I don't think we've had that many cops killed since the police force was organized."

"Well, you've come close a few times."

DeKok shrugged that off.

"Fingerprints, eh?" he mused. He pushed back his chair. "I should be so lucky. What about our own Narcotics Division?"

Vledder gestured vaguely.

"They had *heard* about a Peter Shot. A number of junkies have identified him as a dangerous man, who is always ready to pull a gun. They had also heard that he was a cop-killer in the States. But that was about it. He's never been arrested, either as a user, or as a dealer."

"Did you ask them to keep an eye out?"

Vledder paused, looked at his partner.

"Yes. But do you really think that will serve a purpose?" There was doubt in his voice. "That guy is already somewhere in the Bahamas . . . safe and sound with a tall, cool drink in one hand and a beautiful girl in the other."

DeKok laughed.

"Nevertheless," he said, "it wouldn't do to neglect the possibility. Please make sure they keep an eye out for him . . . don't let them treat it like a routine request."

Vledder was not convinced.

"But why?" he challenged. "Do you really think he'll hang around his abandoned building with his three million?"

DeKok shook his head. There was censure in his look.

"Whoovu, or wherever he may be," he said patiently, "Peter Shot exists. Monika Buwalda mentioned him and Carmen Manouskicheck sold him dope." He paused. "A robbery doesn't just happen. Certainly not a well-planned robbery like the one on the armored car. Peter Shot lived and moved around in Amsterdam. He had connections . . . people who told him about the money transports, routes, weak spots. You understand, plans had to be made . . . people met each other . . . talked to each other. I'm very curious . . ."

One of the other detectives yelled across the room.

Vledder looked up.

"Two guys to see you," yelled the cop near the door.

DeKok motioned for them to proceed.

Two men in faultless, light blue suits approached the desk. DeKok recognized them at once. The two immaculate gentlemen from the funeral. Slowly he rose from his chair.

The two men came closer while DeKok studied them intently. The elegant suits did not match the hard, pitiless, suspicious looks in their eyes.

The smaller of the two reached out a hand.

"My name is Houten," he said with a snobbish accent, "Peter Houten." He glanced aside. "This is Mr. Busil, my partner. We're Directors of the transport company that owns the armored truck that was robbed." He cocked his head at DeKok. "You're Inspector DeKok, is that right?"

"At your service," said DeKok. He gestured to the chairs in front of his desk and sat down himself. The two gentlemen simultaneously pulled up the pants of their trousers to preserve the crease and gingerly lowered themselves in the chairs. Houten rested the tips of his fingers against each other.

"You understand," he began, "that the interests of our Company have been severely damaged. Not only did we lose one

61

of our best employees, but our motto which proclaims that we have developed an infallible system, has lost a lot of credibility."

DeKok nodded resignedly.

"Go on," he said.

Mr. Houten coughed discreetly.

"You should view our visit," he said formally, "as a token of interest. We are very much interested in the results of your investigation."

DeKok smiled brightly.

"There are hardly any . . . results."

Mr. Houten swallowed and brushed an invisible speck of dust from his immaculate trouser leg.

"We are, of course, especially interested in making sure that our Company is not to be blamed in any way. I mean, that we are not guilty of what happened."

DeKok's eyebrows wiggled suddenly. The two gentlemen held their breath and then, in unison shook their head as if to clear their vision. Obviously neither believed the evidence of their eyes. Vledder smirked silently. He had not seem the phenomenon, but knew what had happened by the reaction of the two visitors.

"Is that so?" asked DeKok blandly.

Mr. Busil blushed.

"Every possible precaution has been taken to prevent an event as has happened. We also have extremely reliable, bonded personnel."

DeKok leaned back in his chair.

"You overlooked at least one precaution, didn't you?"

"Whatever do you mean."

"Obviously, it *did* happen, so your precautions were not foolproof."

"Well, . . . eh," sputtered Houten.

"And if your personnel is so reliable, why are they bonded?"

"Because . . . eh," protested Mr. Busil.

"And why," continued DeKok nonchalantly, "did Martin Muller deviate from his assigned route?"

Mr. Houten narrowed his eyes. He had regained some of his composure.

"Who says so?" he asked sharply.

DeKok did not answer. He raised a forefinger in the air and stared at it for a few seconds. Unconsciously the two gentlemen, and even Vledder, found themselves staring at the same finger.

"Martin had no business on Gelder Quay," said DeKok in his most pedantic voice. He paused to let that sink in and then went on: "Which raises, of course, a question that needs to be answered." Before either of the gentlemen could interrupt, DeKok added: "Did he deviate from his route on his own initiative . . . or did either one of you, or you both, order him to deviate from his planned route."

Mr. Busil was angry. He snorted heavily.

"You . . . you," he stammered, "you . . . insinuate that . . ."

DeKok smiled benignly.

"Well Mr. Busil," he invited, "what did I insinuate?"

"That . . . that one of us, *us*, Mr. Houten or myself, had any knowledge of that . . . that, eh . . . dastardly deed."

DeKok smiled again.

"Exactly! But it is not an insinuation, not a suggestion at all. It is merely a recitation of a fact. Martin Muller deviated from his route . . . why?"

Mr. Busil pressed his lips together, he seemed determined not to say another word.

"He did not receive orders to do so," spoke Mr. Houten. "We were extremely surprised ourselves . . . about the robbery . . . and the fact that it happened on Gelder Quay."

"Outside his normal route."

"Indeed."

"Let me repeat my question . . . why?"

Mr. Houten shook his head and Mr. Busil joined him.

"We asked Kees Goor, the other driver, about that," said Mr. Busil. "He only said that Martin suddenly deviated from his route and turned onto Gelder Quay. Before Kees had a chance to protest, the other car had cut them off and he was looking into the barrel of a revolver."

"A revolver, you said?"

"Yes."

DeKok nodded.

"I see, and three million changed ownership."

"That's right."

"Right?"

"No, wrong, of course, but that is what happened."

"I see."

"Well, as I said before. It seems that your personnel is not necessarily as reliable as you claimed . . . bonded, or not." He paused. "Who knew about the amounts to be transported?"

Both Directors remained silent.

DeKok stared at them with that deep, penetrating look that usually made people feel uneasy.

"Who knew about the amounts?" he repeated.

Mr. Busil cleared his throat.

"We . . . eh, we," he said, hesitating, "we had been informed in advance regarding the amounts. We're usually informed, especially if the amount, for whatever reason, is higher than expected. That gives us a chance to take extra precautions."

"And you did not think those necessary in this case?"

Mr. Busil sighed deeply. Houten came to the rescue.

"We discussed it, of course. The city becomes more unsafe by the day. But there is a certain danger in taking extra precautions. The personnel could conclude that an extra large amount was being transported." He made a helpless gesture. "It's impossible for us to keep them from talking."

"You mean that they could inform the criminal element."

"Exactly."

DeKok pulled his lower lip and let it plop back with an audible sound. He repeated the annoying habit several times.

"So . . . you took no special precautions."

"No."

"Because if you had taken extra precautions, your reliable . . . and bonded, personnel could have become less reliable."

"That's absurd," protested Busil.

"Is it?"

"Of course it is."

"Well, we'll leave that aside for now," said DeKok slowly. "But that means that you two were the *only* two that knew that the amount was higher than normal."

Mr. Busil produced a handkerchief and wiped the sweat off his forehead.

"That," he admitted softly, "is a correct assumption."

Mr. Houten had become increasingly more agitated stood up, gesticulating wildly. His face was red and he had trouble articulating.

"What are you trying to do?" he almost screamed. "You *are* accusing us of having something to do with the robbery." He sat down again. "Don't deny it . . . that's what you're saying." He took a deep breath and then continued, slightly calmer. "As Mr. Busil said before . . . that's absurd. Why would we have our own people killed?"

DeKok rose from his chair and hovered over them, a dangerous light in his eyes.

"Not even, Mr. Houten," he hissed, "if the death of Martin Muller clears the way for you to pursue your affair with his wife?"

* * *

Vledder gave his old mentor an admiring look.

"You were in rare form this afternoon," he said enthusiastically. "You really had both of them going. You had them shaking with fear and anger in turn." He grinned boyishly. "At one point I thought Houten was going to attack you."

DeKok nodded slowly.

"Yes, I'm sure it was entertaining." He paused. "And emotional as well. But nevertheless I felt there was a germ of truth in what I said. Now, after his reaction, I'm practically convinced that he is having an affair with the wife of his ex-employee. Martin's death was extremely convenient for our Mr. Houten." He paused again and rubbed his nose. "Let's suppose that Houten has come up with a plan to become rich at a single stroke. An attractive idea and everybody daydreams about that at one time or another. But Mr. Houten happens to be in an extremely well placed position to make his dreams come true. As one of the managers of a firm that moves large amounts of money, he's fully aware when a transport involves an extra large amount. He can also easily direct the truck to a convenient location."

Vledder's eyes lit up.

"Like Gelder Quay."

"Exactly. He instructs the driver to deviate from the regular route. At the same time he makes a deal with a member of the underworld."

Vledder slapped his desk with a flat hand.

"Peter Shot."

DeKok nodded.

"Who, with an accomplice . . ."

"Richard Sloten."

"Right . . . with Richard Sloten cuts off the truck and has special instructions from Houten to shoot down Muller. One inconvenient witness, regarding the changed route, has been eliminated and . . . he now has a free hand with beautiful Ria."

Vledder sat up straight.

"But that's it, DeKok, you've solved it. That's exactly what must have happened. That's . . ." He did not complete the sentence. He gave DeKok a close look. "That . . . eh, your theory. You had that already while we were talking to Houten and Busil?"

DeKok nodded resignedly.

"That's what I used as my starting point."

"But," burst out Vledder, "but then, why didn't you arrest them, or him?"

DeKok gave him a long, hard look.

"I'm lacking just one tiny detail."

"What?"

"Proof."

7

Commissaris* Buitendam, the tall, stately chief of Warmoes Street station, motioned with a slender hand.

"Come in, DeKok," he said in his pretentious voice, "and have a seat." The Commissaris never failed, in his initial contact with his star detective, to attempt a tone of cordial amicability. He made an inviting gesture toward some easy chairs in the corner of his spacious office.

DeKok put on an obstreperous, moody face. His attitude was stubborn and unapproachable, as it usually was when invited by his Chief. For years there had been a barely concealed atmosphere of cautious suspicion between the two. All the more strange since, as DeKok had revealed to Vledder in an unguarded moment, both men had attended the Police Academy together. But where DeKok had pursued the career of a hands-on, street cop, Buitendam had been more political and had eventually wound up as a Commissaris. DeKok's antipathy towards his Chief was not because his former colleague had become a

---

* *Commissaris*: a rank equivalent to Captain. There are only two ranks higher: Chief-Commissaris and Chief Constable. Each jurisdiction has only a single Chief Constable, the highest possible police rank. There is one Chief Constable for all of Amsterdam. Other ranks in the Municipal Police are: Constable, Constable First Class, Sergeant, Adjutant, Inspector, Chief-Inspector and Commissaris. Adjutants and below are equivalent to non-commissioned ranks. Inspector is a rank equivalent to 2nd Lieutenant.

Commissaris, but because he felt, justifiably so, that Buitendam was the wrong man to be in charge of the busy, raucous station. DeKok felt, with many others, that Buitendam would have been of more value in a purely administrative position at Headquarters or, better yet, as a member of the Diplomatic Corps.

In addition, DeKok did not care for anything that he considered as interference with the handling of his cases. The Commissaris, always mindful of the press, superiors and his approaching pension, had a way of interfering that particularly upset DeKok.

"I'd rather stand . . . if it's all the same to you," said DeKok gruffly.

A slight blush colored the pale cheeks of the Commissaris at the rebuke in DeKok's tone.

"As you like," he said and walked back toward his desk. He seated himself behind the desk and placed the tips of his fingers together.

"You're in charge of the investigation into the armored car robbery?"

"Yes."

The Commissaris cleared his throat.

"The Judge-Advocate's office is rather interested in the case," he said. "Maitre Overwhere, the Officer responsible for this district, has called several times requesting progress reports. Of course, I could not tell him more than I had gleaned from Vledder's . . . eh, your preliminary reports. These reports, I must say, were extremely, eh, brief and unenlightening."

DeKok grinned mischievously, but remained silent.

"Well?" urged Buitendam. "Do you have anything to add?"

"I can't report what I don't know."

Buitendam gave his subordinate a searching look.

"I have the distinct feeling, DeKok," he said, feeling his way, "that you . . . as on many occasions in the past . . . give me less than, oh, less than complete information. In other words, you keep information from me . . . deliberately, or otherwise."

DeKok shifted his stance and shrugged.

"It makes no sense," he said brusquely, "to give you long reports full of theories and suppositions that may lead to nothing at all. It's just a waste of time."

The expression on the commissarial face changed. The red in his cheeks became more pronounced and there was a little white line around his nose. He suddenly slammed his fist on the desk.

"From now on I want to be informed on *every* aspect of the case. I want to know every step you take, and I want a complete, you hear complete, report of every interview you conduct." He controlled himself and continued in a calmer tone of voice. "After all, DeKok, it's simply not done that I should have to hear from the Judge-Advocate that you conducted a very indiscreet, I would say ill mannered, yes, ill mannered interview of Mr. Houten, one of the Directors of the firm involved. You made accusations . . . insinuations . . . you were not polite."

DeKok's mouth opened in genuine astonishment.

"What!?" he uttered, dumbfounded.

Buitendam nodded vehemently.

"Mr. Houten filed an official complaint with the Judge-Advocate's Office. He complained about your behavior, your methods, your manners." The Commissaris sounded stern. "He wishes to be spared further contact with you." He pointed at DeKok. "For the record, and with the full knowledge and consent of the Judge-Advocate, you are not to approach either Mr. Houten, or Mr. Busil, from now on. Any interviews or interrogations will be conducted by the Judge-Advocate himself."

DeKok felt his anger rise and controlled it with superhuman effort.

71

"Then I have an immediate task for the Judge-Advocate," spat DeKok.

Buitendam cocked his head.

"Oh?"

"Yes," said DeKok. "Have the Judge-Advocate, in his Judicial Holiness, ask Mr. Houten what he did with the three million."

The Commissaris lost his last shred of patience. Angrily he stood up and pointed at the door.

"OUT!"

* * *

Vledder laughed when DeKok came back to his desk.

"Same story, eh?" The younger man shook his head. "It's about time you learn to be a little more diplomatic. You must have more understanding . . . sympathy."

"What for?"

"For the Commissaris, of course. That man doesn't have an easy life, you know. He has to deal with the Judge-Advocate's Office on a daily basis."

DeKok was still angry.

"Then he should stand up for himself. He should be less of a 'yes' man and more of a man. Sometimes I despair at the use of it all. Some conniving Company Director walks into the Palace of Justice and whines that he has been treated with less respect than his exalted position demands by some poor, hard-working Inspector of Police. Right-a-way all the big guns are brought into action and steps are taken."

Vledder looked nonplussed.

"Steps taken?"

"Yes," nodded DeKok. "We'll have to discuss every step in this case beforehand with the Commissaris and we're especially

72

prohibited from approaching Mr. Houten in any way, shape, or form."

"We can't interrogate him further?"

"That's right."

Vledder was amazed.

"Really? So . . . who will do that?"

"The Judge-Advocate himself."

Vledder grimaced.

"Well, in that case we can forget all about 'proof' for the time being." He grinned again, full of disbelief. "How on earth can the man make that kind of decision? What chances does a man like that have during an interrogation? He knows nothing about the various aspects we encounter during the daily process of such an investigation. . . all those subtle hints that, perhaps, may not constitute legal evidence, but that become extremely important in order to arrive at an overall conclusion."

DeKok looked at his assistant with admiration.

"Dick," he said with feeling, "you're starting to think like a real cop . . . not a bureaucrat." He laughed. "It won't be long now, and I can retire."

Vledder waved away all praise.

"I'm serious," he said. "I'm starting to get real mixed feelings about *the investigating officer of choice*, as they so loftily describe the Judge-Advocate in the Law books."

DeKok curled his lips.

"As long as they don't think," he said, popping a peppermint into his mouth, "that I will leave the gentlemen of that Company in peace." It sounded threatening. "If they are involved in these murders, I will prove it . . . whether the Judge-Advocate likes it, or not." He paused, a twinkle in his eyes. "According to the Commissaris I have real trouble remembering instructions and . . ."

DeKok stopped and stared across the room. Little Lowee had entered at the far end. With a disdainful gesture the small barkeeper ignored the cop near the door and barged right through the confusion in the room towards DeKok's desk.

DeKok immediately rose from behind his desk and welcomed his friend heartily.

"Lowee," he said, surprise in his voice, "you've left your . . . eh, your establishment!"

Little Lowee smiled shyly. He tossed his head in the direction of the door.

"Cross-eyed Jack is holdin' da fort. Tha's why I cain't stay long or he'll drink all me stuff."

DeKok gave him a probing look. He knew that the diminutive barkeeper did not like visiting the station. He was afraid people would brand him as an informer. He was, of course, but only for DeKok and he always refused to take any money for the information he shared with his old friend.

"Something the matter?" asked DeKok, concerned.

"You still wanna find Peter Shot?"

"Yes, I do."

"They done seen 'im."

"Who?"

Lowee hesitated, glanced at Vledder. Vledder took the hint and busied himself with his computer terminal. The beeps from the screen and the clacking of the keyboard, added to the normal noise of the room, formed an effective sound screen. Even so, Lowee leaned closer and whispered.

"Two of da guys . . . guys that come in me place."

"When did they see him?"

"About a week ago."

"Where?"

"Short King Street. Peter looked real bad, they says. He was drunk or somethin'. He wuz witta guy and a broad. They sorta held him up."

"Supported him?"

"Tha's what I says."

"What time was that?"

"After midnight."

"Where did they go?"

Lowee shrugged.

"They went inna way to Ol' Fort."

"The canal?"

"Nah, the street."

DeKok looked pensive.

"What did the man and the woman look like?"

Lowee made a helpless gesture.

"Geez, DeKok, I don't know. You see, itsa only hearsay, you knows. I didna see them meself. Da guys only looked atta broad. Some piece they says. Veenoos Demeelo but wiv everythin' workin', you knows?"

DeKok rubbed his chin, nodding.

"I better not ask you who the two guys were, who told you that."

Lowee laughed uneasily.

"I gotta think of me customers . . . and me reputacy."

DeKok nodded his understanding. He walked Lowee back to the lobby downstairs and patted him on the shoulder.

"Thanks again, Lowee." he said.

He remained in the lobby for a few moments and watched Lowee disappear toward Corner Alley. Then he turned around and climbed the stairs back to the detective room.

Vledder was still behind his desk.

"Well?" asked Vledder.

"Well, what?"

"You think Lowee's information was important?"

DeKok pushed his lower lip forward, then pulled it and let it plop back. He repeated the annoying motion several times.

"We'll see," he said, not committing himself.

Vledder waved a hand.

"Seems pretty straightforward to me. After discussing the robbery one more time, they had a few drinks and Richard Sloten and his . . . eh, his fiancee, took Peter home."

DeKok nodded slowly.

"That's the way it could have been."

DeKok's telephone rang. Vledder reached over and answered it. After a few moments he replaced the receiver and looked confused.

"What is it?" asked DeKok.

"I'm not sure. Mrs. Sloten wasn't at the funeral."

"Her son's funeral?"

"Yes."

"When was that?"

"Now."

DeKok reflected.

"Who was that on the line?" he asked.

"Stoops."

"Mark Stoops?"

"Yes," said Vledder. "You know," he continued apologetically, "that I don't like cemeteries. Therefore I asked Stoops to attend the funeral, to check the seals and such. I told him which people were likely to show up and to make a report of those that actually did, or did not. Stoops is an excellent cop and I thought . . ."

DeKok did not listen any further. He turned on his heels and grabbed raincoat and hat from the peg as he rushed toward the door. Vledder was right behind him.

"Where to now?" asked Vledder, catching up.

76

"Triangle Street," said DeKok, racing down the stairs. "Perhaps we won't be too late."

* * *

Vledder whipped the old VW along the narrow streets with screeching tires and blaring siren. For once DeKok did not object to the noise. He contemplated the fleeting scenery with a somber expression on his face. He suddenly realized both the daring of, and the danger from, his unknown, merciless opponent.

Vledder glanced aside.

"Perhaps she didn't know," he said.

"What?"

"The exact time."

DeKok did not react. It was a stupid remark, but he understood how Vledder felt.

There was no parking spot available and Vledder came as close as he could, squeezed the car between some other cars and parked on the sidewalk. Together they ran toward the address in Triangle Street. For once Vledder saw nothing amusing in DeKok at speed and DeKok ignored the picturesque, restored facades. He smacked open the front door and climbed the narrow, creaking stairs with amazing agility and speed.

The apartment door upstairs was closed. DeKok felt the doorknob and as it gave under the pressure, he cautiously pushed the door wider.

She was on the carpet, next to a tall, slender chair with bowed legs. There was a slight bulge on the back of the black kimono and one of her slippers had come off a foot.

DeKok knelt next to her and felt for the neck artery. Vledder watched tensely.

"Dead?" he asked finally.

DeKok nodded slowly.

"Murdered," he said, "alert the *Herd*."

8

Dark clots of blood stuck to the graying hair. Carefully DeKok wiped some of the hair away. Near the neck vertebrae, close together, were two black rimmed gunshot wounds. A thin trickle of coagulated blood ran down to her chin. It had formed a little puddle on the carpet.

Vledder swallowed.

"Neck shots. Just like Richard Sloten and Martin Muller."

DeKok nodded grimly.

"The trademark of this particular killer."

Slowly, with effort, he rose from his kneeling position. His knees creaked. He looked down at the victim. She did not have a chance, he thought. He gestured toward Vledder.

"What about the *Herd*?"

With a start Vledder came back to the present and realized that it was the second time DeKok had told him to alert the small army of experts that always gathered at the scene of a violent crime. *Thundering Herd* was DeKok's special name for this gathering.

As soon as Vledder had left, DeKok, without touching anything, let his eyes roam around the room. Carefully he observed and stored the information in his remarkable memory. He had developed a near photographic memory during his long career and he preferably trusted his first impressions above all others. Not a detail, no matter how small, escaped his scrutiny.

The room looked almost the same as the last time he had seen it, a few days ago. This time there was a small silver vase with white orchids next to the color photograph of Richard Sloten.

DeKok kept staring at it. The sight touched him. The two white orchids conveyed a sense of intense grief. Their chilly, distant beauty conveyed a message of such infinite sadness, that a chill ran up and down his spine. Suddenly he realized how much the woman had loved her son. A love the son had spurned. He had not availed himself of the comfort and nurturing that love could have provided him. Abruptly DeKok realized he had failed. His self-castigation was like a physical pain. He should have come himself. He should never have left it to others to inform the dead woman of the horrible death of her son in faraway Drente.

His gaze travelled to the floor, to the dead woman in her silk kimono. If he had been here, at the time, he might have been able to get more information from her. The notification in itself might have elicited further confidences, might have induced her to be more furthcoming. Perhaps, in the grip of her grief, she might have talked about the things she had kept to herself before. Perhaps she could have told him more about Peter Shot, his accomplices, the macabre dancers around the golden calf of three million.

With a deep sigh he came to grips, not for the first time, with the realization that most of life was a series of "could have beens" and missed opportunities.

The return of Vledder interrupted his musing.

"They're coming," said Vledder, pointing over his shoulder.

Bram Weelen, the police photographer, was the first to arrive. He placed his aluminum suitcase just outside the door and started to assemble his Hasselblad. Meanwhile he glanced at DeKok.

"Another problem?"

DeKok shook hands with Weelen and smiled.

"It's my profession."

Bram Weelen nodded agreement.

"The usual? Or do you have special wishes?"

DeKok nodded. He pointed at the portrait, flanked by the orchids.

"I want a special close-up of that."

Weelen nodded carelessly

"Your wish is my command," he said. He aimed his camera at the still-life. Suddenly he lowered the instrument and looked at DeKok. "But why?"

A tired smile crossed over DeKok's face.

"For sentimental reasons. That's all. The boy in the picture is her only son. He was murdered four days ago."

Weelen was taken aback.

"The guy from the robbery?"

DeKok nodded. He pointed at the corpse.

"I was here less than four days ago. In this same room. If she had told me everything then, she could still be alive today."

"Had her son already been killed at that time?"

"No," shook DeKok. "At least I didn't know it yet. I was here a few hours after the robbery. Ben Kruger had just identified some of the prints on the getaway car as those belonging to her son."

Weelen grunted in assent.

"Any news of Peter Shot?"

DeKok sighed.

"Not a trace."

81

Vledder pointed at the corpse, a grim smile on his face.

"You can hardly call it 'without a trace,' " he said. "There is his business card."

DeKok did not appreciate the remark, but he did not respond. Weelen again aimed his camera. The flashes illuminated the room.

An old, small man appeared in the door opening. Behind him, on the landing, they could see two men in the uniform of morgue attendants. The small man remained on the threshold, a pince-nez balanced precariously on his nose. He was dressed in striped trousers and a black, cut-away coat. A large, floppy, greenish Garibaldi hat was in one hand.

DeKok moved toward the door. He shook the man's hand.

"Dr. Koning," he exclaimed, "not retired yet?"

The old Coroner made a defensive movement.

"Rest rusts," he said in a creaky voice. "I'd rather keep on the move." He pushed the pince-nez firmer on his nose. "And the more corpses I encounter, the more I realize how precious life really is."

DeKok nodded sympathetically. He liked the old Coroner. They had known each other for what seemed like an eternity, but always seemed to meet under the most macabre circumstances. With a start DeKok remembered that at one time the old man had actually been a suspect in a murder case.*

"Your patient," said DeKok, pointing at the corpse.

Dr. Koning came closer. He pulled up the legs of his striped trouser and knelt down. He turned the body slightly and looked at the face. Both eyes were swollen and the nose had been flattened by the carpet. Carefully he lowered the shoulder and then he

---

*See: DeKok and the Romantic Murder.

stared for some time at the two gunshot wounds in the neck. With difficulty he rose to a standing position.

"She's dead," he announced.

"Thank you, doctor," said DeKok formally, accepting the official pronouncement for the record. Then he said: "We're very interested in the time of death."

Dr. Koning removed a handkerchief from his breast pocket and proceeded to clean his glasses. He gave DeKok a disapproving look as he did so.

"Really, DeKok," said the old doctor, "you know better than anyone that I do not like to give opinions at the crime site."

"Indulge me, doctor," wheedled DeKok.

"As usual," grumped the doctor. He replaced the handkerchief and the pince-nez. He looked sternly at DeKok. "Please keep in mind that this is unofficial and *must* be confirmed by a regular autopsy."

"Yes, doctor," agreed DeKok readily.

"Well, I estimate she died at least two days ago."

DeKok looked startled.

"Two days!?"

The Coroner nodded.

"Perhaps three days." He adjusted his glasses until they again wobbled precariously on his nose. He looked at DeKok over the top of them.

"Please advise whoever does the autopsy to look for the bullets. There are no exit wounds. The bullets are probably lodged in the brain."

DeKok looked pensive.

"Then she was shot from below."

"Indeed."

"The path of the bullets is in an upward direction," continued DeKok. "That means that she was standing up and that the killer approached her from behind and then shot her."

Dr. Koning nodded slowly.

"Yes, and from close by. He lifted the weapon and almost touched the skin."

DeKok stared into the distance.

"A cowardly killer."

Dr. Koning looked up in surprise.

"You're right," he said after a slight pause, "a cowardly killer. He was afraid to look her in the eyes." The old Coroner looked once more at the victim. Then he pressed his old Garibaldi hat back on his head. He gave DeKok a bitter smile. "But the killer," he concluded, "the killer . . . is your problem."

They shook hands formally and the old man left.

DeKok glanced at Weelen, who nodded. He had taken all the pictures he needed. With another glance DeKok alerted the morgue attendants. They approached and with routine movements they placed the body in the body bag and then on the stretcher. They carried it off.

DeKok watched as they manoeuvred the stretcher down the narrow stairs. After a while he heard the doors of the morgue vehicle slam shut and he turned to Vledder.

"Who notified her of the death of her son?"

"Stoops."

"I see."

Vledder nodded, still upset by his own, perceived lack of attention to detail.

"You see," Vledder explained further, "that's why Stoops called at once when he did not see her at the funeral. He knew she had no other relatives and he had intended to stand by her, at the funeral, if that were needed."

DeKok nodded. He knew Stoops as a compassionate cop.

"How did he know about the relatives?"

"She told him herself," said Vledder.

"What else?"

Vledder looked puzzled.

"What . . . what else?"

"What else did she tell him."

Vledder shrugged his shoulders.

"I'm not sure. I didn't ask. But apparently they talked for some time."

DeKok looked at the busy scurrying of a number of technicians, then he turned toward Weelen.

"Where's Ben Kruger?"

The photographer smiled.

"I knew you wanted him," he said. "he'll be along in a moment. He was held up on another assignment."

The words were barely out of his mouth, when the fingerprint expert came up the stairs.

"Speak of the devil . . ." said Weelen.

DeKok greeted Kruger and waved at Weelen as the latter descended the stairs.

"You'll have the pictures tomorrow," called Weelen from downstairs.

Kruger wiped the sweat off his forehead.

"I don't know if I shouldn't have walked," he complained. "Traffic is getting worse by the day. I've spent more time in gridlock today, than anywhere else. Maybe they should ban cars altogether from the inner city." He looked around. "What happened here?"

DeKok pointed at the bloodstain on the carpet.

"A woman was murdered."

"Armed robbery"

DeKok shook his head.

"I don't think so. I think she knew too much . . . she was dangerous to somebody."

"And what do you need from me?"

"A lot, Ben, quite a lot. I want more than the routine search for prints. I want to find *every* print in the house, wherever you can find them . . . the kitchen, the bathroom, inside cupboards . . . everywhere. Excluding the prints of the dead woman and her son, I will be extremely interested in whatever else you can find."

"The son?"

"He was killed a few days ago. He should be in your files. The body of the woman is in the morgue and if you don't have her prints, you can get them there. Vledder will fill you in on all the details."

"That will take some time," protested Kruger, "everything in the house?"

"Yes."

"Oh, well, you'll have your reasons, I suppose."

"I hope so," said DeKok.

"Well," said Kruger, "I better get started. Anyplace you're through?" he asked one of the technicians who was gathering samples of various items.

"We're through in the kitchen, sir," said the technician in a pleasant contralto voice.

Kruger took a second look. The formless coveralls of the Technical Service could barely disguise the shapely form of the woman.

"I'm getting old," Kruger said.

The fingerprint expert disappeared into the kitchen and DeKok watched him go with a smile. He liked the old dactyloscopist. Nothing ever seemed too much trouble for him. Vledder rummaged through some papers he had found in a drawer. Again DeKok was struck by the orchids next to the portrait. Suddenly he caught his breath.

"The doll," he exclaimed loudly.

Everyone in the room stopped what they were doing and looked at him.

"The doll in the costume," clarified DeKok.

"What's the matter with it?" asked Vledder.

"It's gone."

9

Vledder sealed the premises. First he strung yellow tape crosswise across the door and then he connected the intersection of the tape to the doorknob with a nylon string. The knot in the string was covered with a clump of sealing wax into which he pressed the official police seal. Inside, almost every surface was covered with the greasy aluminum powder used by Kruger who had left without much hope. As usual in a Dutch home, everything had been painfully clean and his harvest of usable prints had been meager.

Vledder checked the seal one more time and then descended the stairs, From Triangle Street he walked to the corner of Palm Canal.

DeKok was already in the car. He was sprawled in the passenger seat, his hat pressed down over his eyes. His thoughts went over the most recent murder and he chastised himself for having failed, for not having prevented this latest killing. DeKok was his own worst critic.

Vledder slid behind the wheel, started the engine and extricated the car from its unorthodox parking spot. The old VW groaned when Vledder stepped on the brakes just in time, as the light jumped on red. DeKok banged his head against the windshield and his hat fell off.

"A little less banging around, please," he said mildly. "I'd like to reach my retirement in one piece."

Vledder blushed.

"I . . . I was thinking of something else," he admitted.

DeKok retrieved his hat.

"What about?"

The light changed to green and Vledder put the car back in motion.

"That doll. I can't figure it. Do you think the doll has anything to do with the motive for the murder?"

DeKok gingerly felt his forehead.

"If it starts to swell, you'll have to explain it to my wife."

Vledder was irritated.

"The doll . . . could it be a motive?"

DeKok shrugged.

"The only thing we know for sure is that the doll was still there, four days ago. And now it's gone."

"You think the killer took it?"

"It looks that way. I can't think of a single reason why Mrs. Sloten would have removed the doll herself. It was an expensive doll. Very decorative. Anyway . . . I looked all over the house for it and it's not there." He looked at Vledder. "Anything among the papers?"

Vledder shook his head, not taking his eyes off the road.

"Nothing . . . at least nothing we can use. Just the usual stuff . . . letters, insurance papers, some photos. Apparently the killer was not after money. There was more than a thousand in cash, plus a checkbook, some credit cards and all the necessary identification papers." He grinned without joy. "It seems more than likely that Peter Shot is responsible for this killing as well. With three million in your possession, you don't need small change."

DeKok grunted something unintelligible.

90

They drove for a long time in silence. Vledder's stomach growled. It was already past six o'clock and his attention to the road was diverted by visions of food. He found himself daydreaming about a *rijsttafel*, that subtle combination of Dutch and Indonesian cuisine, washed down with several bottles of beer. He was just about to turn the car in the direction of one of their favorite restaurants, when DeKok spoke up.

"You Have Monika Buwalda's address?"

"Of course," answered Vledder, changing direction for Warmoes Street. "She lives in Dovecote, in the suburbs."

"Really? Where?"

"In an apartment building."

"You're just a mine of information. Can you be more specific?"

Vledder did not answer at once. He drove a short distance into Warmoes Street and parked in front of the station house. Then he pulled his notebook out of his pocket and flipped a few pages.

"The building is called *Hickory* and it's on Poplar Street." he replaced the notebook in his pocket. "What do you want?" he asked curtly. "You want her to come to the station?"

DeKok shook his head.

"No, we're going to visit *her*."

* * *

Monika was dressed in a long, flowing, pink creation that did little to conceal her exquisite figure. On her feet were delicate bedroom slippers with stiletto heels. She looked bewitching. Again DeKok savored the aroma of her exciting perfume.

In about the center of the room, she fluffed up a purple bean bag and lowered herself in a graceful movement. A shapely leg peeked from the translucent material. The old Inspector lowered

91

himself cautiously into something that most resembled a small hammock on four spindly legs. When the contraption seemed to be able to carry his weight, he took a closer look at his hostess. The long, blonde hair had lost none of its sparkle. It bobbed gently with every movement of her head. The luscious skin was tight and rounded in all the right places and the same confusing, exotic light beamed from her eyes.

DeKok smiled faintly to himself. Monika Buwalda did not at all look like a young woman who had just buried her dearly beloved. For some strange reason it did not surprise him.

As he contemplated the exquisite woman, Vledder suddenly started the conversation. He was uncomfortably perched on the edge of a hassock.

"Our investigations into Peter Shot," began Vledder, "have so far been without any results. Even his real name has eluded us. Apparently Peter Shot has completely disappeared from the surface of the earth."

Monika gave him a mocking look.

"And you're surprised about that . . . with three million? Of course Peter has long since escaped to a foreign country."

Vledder swallowed.

"We have reason to believe that he is still in Holland."

She narrowed her eyes.

"Where?"

Vledder smiled.

"That's exactly the question I wanted to ask you."

"Me?"

Vledder nodded with conviction.

"There are witnesses who have seen you . . . with Peter Shot."

"When?"

"A few days before the robbery."

She smiled and Vledder shook with confusion and sudden arousal. The look on her face would have brought a statue to life. He moved uneasily on the edge of his seat, trying to control himself.

"But I already told your colleague," she said sweetly, with a hint of promise in her sexy voice that made Vledder even more uncomfortable. "Richard and Peter planned things ... had discussions. I was there at a few of the meetings."

Vledder tore his gaze away from the temptress. He settled his eyes on a point just above her head. His hands balled into fists and his nails pressed into the palms of his hands. With an effort he resisted the urge to loosen his collar.

"On the occasion the witnesses mentioned," he said huskily, "it seemed that Peter Shot was drunk. He staggered between you and another man."

For a moment Monika lost her poise, her eyes flickered and a slight blush appeared on her cheeks. Then she opened her mouth slightly and her tongue flicked out, wetting her lips. She smiled again and then she turned her full gaze once more on Vledder.

"Where was that?" she asked breathlessly.

For a moment Vledder lowered his eyes and looked in her face. He felt his personality disappear into the liquid pools of her eyes. He felt hypnotized. When he spoke again, his voice was hoarse.

"In Short King Street . . . just after midnight."

Monika grabbed her knees and leaned back, jutting out her breasts. A clear, melodious laugh escaped as she threw back her head in apparent abandon. By averting her eyes, she gave Vledder the opportunity to recover a little. Again he looked at the space over her head. She leaned forward.

"That's right," she said cheerily. "I remember now. Peter did not even drink all that much, that night. But I think he may

93

have used some dope before we met him. In the beginning he was very enthusiastic, happy, almost exuberant. But after his third drink he became drowsy and started to spout nonsense." She waved a graceful hand, as if dismissing a minion. "Drugs, in combination with alcohol have a more intense effect."

Vledder nodded to himself, still avoiding her gaze.

"Where did you take him? As far as we know, Peter Shot has no permanent address in Amsterdam . . . never did."

Monika moved in her seat. The dress fell away on both sides of her body as she brought her knees and ankles together. She placed her hands on the bag next to her and sat up straight. Except for the flimsy material covering her breasts, she was totally nude and exposed. But her position and the shape of the bean bag created tantalizing shadows and concealed hidden charms from obvious view. Vledder was aware of what was happening, but kept his gaze resolutely averted. DeKok silently watched her eyes only. She took a deep breath, straining the material of her dress even more.

"Peter," she said finally, hesitatingly, searching for the words, "At that time Peter lived under an assumed name in a . . . eh, a small hotel . . . somewhere on Martyrs Canal, not too far from New Dike. I . . . eh, I do not remember the name of the hotel," she added with an apologetic smile that did not reach her eyes. "But," she added in a seductive voice, "I could go there with you . . . to show you." She lowered her head and looked at Vledder from beneath long eyelashes. "I am good at showing places . . . and things," she continued. "For years I worked as a hostess for a large company. Would you like me to show you?"

Silently Vledder screamed yes as he rubbed the back of his neck. DeKok coughed discreetly. With a startled glance at his partner, Vledder again returned to reality. He felt like he was in a dream. From a distance he heard his own questions and her answers, but the substance did not seem to penetrate his flustered mind.

"You took Peter to the hotel?" he asked, finally.

She nodded.

"Together with Richard."

Vledder pressed his lips together. He looked at her, but quickly looked away.

"Do you realize," he spoke to the space above her head, "that it is almost certain that that same Peter Shot murdered Richard?"

Monika nodded again. The same mysterious, promising smile on her lips.

"I realize that," she said.

A slow irritation was beginning to affect Vledder, lessening her bewitching spell. He shuffled his feet. He realized that anger was the best defense against her exciting presence. But anger was also the worst enemy of the investigating cop. He controlled himself as best as possible. But there was agitation in his voice when next he spoke.

"I don't get the impression," he said harshly, "that you're very upset by the death of your . . . eh, your fiancee."

Monika's face fell. Her challenging attitude seemed to disappear and she pushed out her lower lip in a pouting gesture that did nothing to diminish the sexual attraction of both her figure and her position.

"How can a hard, insensitive policeman, like you," she said with a sob in her voice, "gauge the sorrow of a woman like myself?"

Vledder came to his feet, stung to the core.

"Insensitive, insensitive," he blustered, his voice breaking. "I know only one insensitive . . ."

DeKok intervened. He stretched out a hand toward his partner and made a soothing gesture.

"You should not jump to conclusions," he said patiently. "Women are very capable of masking their grief, their true feelings. Personally I'm convinced that Richard's passing has touched Ms. Buwalda deeply."

She gave DeKok a grateful look.

"Richard and I loved each other."

DeKok nodded calmly.

"And that . . . is why," he said, "I'm so extremely sorry to have to tell you about the death of Richard's mother."

Her almond shaped eyes became wide and she turned full towards him, parting the last remaining covering of her breasts.

"Richard's mother . . . dead?"

DeKok looked at her coolly, unaffected by the nearly naked woman.

"Murdered . . . two shots in the neck."

Monika paled. She closed her eyes and both hands went to her forehead. She tried to get up and stumbled. Then she collapsed backward. Her legs were spread and her arms were flung away from her body. The totally exposed, naked figure was sprawled supine across the bean bag like the sacrifice of an ancient rite, offered on a lumpy altar.

10

DeKok had tired feet.

With a painful grimace he lifted his feet from the floor and carefully placed them on top of his desk. It felt as if thousands of small devils used his calves as a pincushion for their pitchforks. It was a bad sign, he knew. Whenever a case was not proceeding according to plan, when he seemed to be further away from the solution, rather than closer to it, the tiredness would flow into his feet and the little devils started their satanic torture. He knew that the pain was psychosomatic, but that did not make it any less real.

The most disturbing aspect of the killings was that they were not *Dutch* enough. It was not usual for a Dutchman to finish off his victim with neck shots. He had never before encountered it in his long career. It was just too impersonal, too inhuman. Although he was convinced that murder was strictly a *human* occupation, he also felt that most murders were the result of passion, of the heat of the moment. But these murders resembled too much an execution, they were outside his experience. He could not *feel* them.

He shook his head in a vain attempt to clear it and to forget the pain in his legs. What drove the killer to murder Martin Muller, Richard Sloten and his mother, one after the other? Who was Peter Shot? A non-Dutch killer? What role was being played by Houten and Busil? Were they the brains behind the robbery? And what about Monika Buwalda? She could certainly faint most enticingly and had been close to confusing Vledder past the point of discretion. Why did the killer have an interest in a doll, a doll in the costume of some eastern country? And most of all . . . where was the three million?

The questions seemed to overwhelm him and the hellish pain in his legs distracted him from finding the answers. He and Vledder had been working on the case for almost a week and they were no closer to a solution.

Vledder, who knew the symptoms and their implications, gave DeKok a concerned look.

"Tired feet?"

DeKok laboriously lifted his right leg and felt his calves.

"It must be genetic," he complained. He sighed deeply and replaced the leg on the desk. "My old grandmother had the same problem. I used to spend a lot of time with her when I was a child and I knew all her moods and peculiarities. When there was bad weather in the offing, she would complain of tired feet, but what she described is exactly what I feel." He smiled at the memory. "My grandfather fished on what used to be the Zuyder Zee . . . under sail, you understand. Engines were unheard of . . . or rarely. They were just cockleshells, those fishing smacks from then. It was always a blessing and a miracle when they returned to port."

Vledder listened spell-bound. Rarely did DeKok talk about his early days.

"My granny could take one look at the sky," he continued, "and no matter how promising the weather looked to you, or me, she could always tell. When she sat down closer to the fire and placed her wrap around her and complain about tired feet, you knew we were in for a blow." DeKok stared into the distance. "I can still see her, the old lady . . . a weathered skin with thousands of tiny laugh wrinkles . . . the colorful costume of the island, Urk, you know, and her crooked, arthritic hands folded in her pinafore, praying for the safekeeping of the fleet."

He rubbed his legs.

"Because that God was her guide and her strength she confessed openly and without shame. And when she went to bed at night and took off her outer clothes and her many petticoats, there was but little left of her. But I always felt safe with her, although I was almost as tall as she was. But I loved it best on Sunday, when she put on her Sunday costume with the large gold ornaments and the big hood that reminded one of a nun. Then she was beautiful beyond compare. In my eyes she was a queen striding forth with the old family Bible in one hand and my fist in the other. To me she seemed so impressive that I always wondered that people did not line the streets and applaud us as we passed. The national costume of Urker women is formal and magnificent. Of all the costumes in the world . . ."

He stopped suddenly. The dreamy look disappeared from his eyes. He lifted his legs from the desk and with hardly a stumble he walked over to the coat rack.

"What about your feet?" asked Vledder, returning with a shock from the Zuyder Zee of so long ago.

DeKok motioned to him.

"Over," he said.

Vledder rose and joined him.

"Where are we going?"

DeKok hoisted himself into his raincoat while he walked toward the door. Then he put his hat on his head.

"We're off to North Market."

"Why?"

The gray sleuth smiled.

"Peter Karstens."

Vledder looked disapproving.

"That forger, that painter who breaks every law made by God and man?"

DeKok raised a finger in the air.

"A gifted artist," he corrected.

* * *

From Warmoes Street they passed through Old Bridge Alley toward New Dijk. It was busy in the District, as usual. Crowds of tourists invaded the Red Light District, Amsterdam's famous Quarter. One of the foremost attractions in the minds of many. DeKok pulled up the collar of his raincoat. The night air was chilly.

"No news of that blue car . . . the whatever."

Vledder shook his head.

"The Jaguar. No, I've not received any response to my request for information. I was thinking of having something mentioned in the papers . . . but, of course, we need permission from the commissaris for that. It might help. We can decide that later. Meanwhile the State Police have forwarded the impressions of the tires and they were kind enough to match them. The marks found in Drente definitely match those found where we assume the exchange of cars took place. Not a doubt. The same car."

"The bullets?"

"I only have one from Doldersum. The second bullet exited the body. They tried, but so far have been unable to locate it on that sandy path. But the one bullet we have *does* match the bullets recovered from Martin Muller."

DeKok nodded.

"And the bullets from Mrs. Sloten?"

"Too early as of yet. That is, I have no official report. But a friend at the lab told me that the bullets will more than likely match on all points."

"A revolver?"

"Yes, Peter Shot's revolver. But then, we were almost sure it was a revolver when we didn't find any shells."

"Yes, yes," said DeKok, "I was just thinking out loud."

In silence they walked on.

It started to rain. A miserable, ground-soaking drizzle that seems to be invented just for Amsterdam. DeKok pulled his hat deeper over his eyes and hunched his shoulders. From Emperors Canal they crossed the bridge toward Princes Street and from there along a short length of Prince's Canal toward North Market. Behind the Reformed Church, they stopped in front of a small house with a big, high window. In the middle of the window were the words *Peter Karstens* in elegant scroll lettering. Underneath, in smaller letters, he read: *Painter- Artist.*

"What do you want from him?"

"A painting," answered DeKok.

"An imitation Monet . . . for your living room?" grinned Vledder.

DeKok did not answer, but looked at his watch. It was after ten. With relish he gave a yank on the brass bell pull. Inside the house he heard the rattle of the bell, loud and insistent. DeKok was not worried about the noise. He had known the occupant for a long time and knew his nocturnal habits. For years there had been a love-hate relationship between the artist and the cop, tempered by mutual respect and genuine affection. DeKok had a lot of ambiguous acquaintances like that.

It took about two minutes and then the door was opened by a man with dark-blond hair, dressed in sweat pants and a tee shirt. He frowned until he recognized DeKok.

101

"DeKok," exclaimed the man with a mixture of surprise and delight. "Again?"

The Inspector nodded slowly.

"Yes, you helped me so splendidly on a prior occasion that I thought I might call on you again."

"I don't feel much like turning into a regular accomplice of the police," growled Karstens.

DeKok waved that away.

"It's raining, Pete, let us in."

For just a moment the artist hesitated, then a smile came on his face and he opened his arms wide.

"Of course, come in." He looked at Vledder. "I see you brought your accomplice with you."

DeKok cocked his head.

"The police have no accomplices," he said, "the police have colleagues, or partners."

Peter Karstens grinned broadly.

"What about criminal accomplices . . . are they partners, or colleagues?"

DeKok shook his head with a mock gesture of despair. Karstens led the way through the showroom and main studio to a set of stairs in the back. A short corridor at the bottom led to a spacious room with a low ceiling supported by heavy beams. The room was comfortably furnished with couches, a large round table and several easy chairs. The walls were covered with books and paintings and spotlights were scattered around the room between the furniture. An easel stood to one side.

DeKok looked around for the beautiful woman who had been living with the painter for years.*

"She's not here?" he asked, disappointment in his voice.

---

*See: *DeKok and Murder in Seance.*

The artist shook his head, a twinkle in his eyes.

"No, Maria went to visit her mother." He shrugged. "Every Thursday. She calls it a social obligation."

DeKok looked at the large table. A set of exquisite goblets sparkled in the light of several candles. The goblets were clean and empty.

"No wine?"

"I don't drink alone," answered Karstens. "Wine is to be enjoyed in good company. And since Maria went to her mother . . ." He did not finish the sentence, but winked at the two cops. "But since you're here, I'll be happy to open a bottle."

DeKok sat down in a rattan chair and watched as the artist opened a bottle of red wine and filled the goblets. The yellow candlelight helped to create a festive atmosphere.

"I want you to paint a woman for me," said DeKok.

Peter was surprised.

"A woman . . . what woman?"

DeKok laughed.

"Just a woman," he repeated. "Use Maria as a model, although she certainly is not *just* a woman. But paint her in a specific costume."

"What sort of costume?"

"A national costume." DeKok rubbed the back of his neck. "That's the problem. I have only seen it once and I can give you a description, but I have no idea to what region or country the costume belongs. But, after I give you the description, I would like you to paint it. I can't pay you and the painting will remain, of course, your property. I just need it for a while during my investigations."

Peter Karstens handed him a goblet.

"What investigations?"

DeKok did not answer at once. Slowly he moved the goblet closer to his lips and sniffed the aroma. A Burgundy, he concluded. The wine was like velvet and he gave it the proper attention. He drained about half of it and then placed the glass back on the table.

"The robbery of the armored car."

"Those three million?"

"Yes."

Peter Karstens looked at him, a faint smile on his face.

"You're involved with that?"

"Yes."

"That's more than a week, isn't it?"

"Yes."

Peter Karstens leaned back, his glass in one hand and his other pointing at the ceiling.

"You know, DeKok, I almost committed that robbery."

Vledder coughed suddenly. The statement had caused him to swallow a sip of wine that went down the wrong way. He placed his glass on the table and took several deep breaths. Karstens and DeKok looked at him, but Vledder shook his head, indicating he was all right. As Karstens again looked at DeKok, Vledder unobtrusively slipped his notebook out of his pocket and balanced it on one knee. He started to take notes.

The interruption had given DeKok time to recover from the amazing statement by the artist.

"Are you serious?" he asked.

Karstens nodded, still smiling.

"Of course I'm serious. It was a perfect plan . . . very clever and at the same time very simple. Frankly, I'm surprised nobody else ever thought of it before."

DeKok was confused.

"What plan?"

Karstens leaned forward.

"A second truck." He waved a hand in the air. "A second truck, painted exactly like the first one, the real one." He stood up and walked over to a sideboard. From a drawer he pulled some photos and handed them to DeKok.

DeKok looked at the photos, before passing them on to Vledder. They were color photos of the truck that had been blocked on Gelder Quay. The truck had been photographed in great detail and from all angles.

Karstens leaned over DeKok.

"You see, I already made these pictures. I followed that truck for weeks and I knew exactly what the drivers did at each stop . . . their route . . . the estimated value of each pick-up." He tapped the pictures with a long forefinger. "Those trucks are manufactured in France. They're just very expensive . . . too expensive. I just couldn't raise the cash to buy one."

Vledder was studying the photos as DeKok looked at Karstens, a calculating look in his eyes.

"How had you planned to proceed?"

Peter resumed his seat.

"There are a couple of weak spots in the route of that particular truck. Right after it leaves the depot it has to get through some narrow streets. It would be easy to create a pile up at that time. You just have a car break down in front of the truck. It would take almost an hour before you could even get a tow truck in there." He laughed out loud. "At the same time you follow the route with the fake truck. It only takes about forty-three minutes from that time and you have your truck full with all the pick-ups from that day." Peter paused again and laughed boyishly. "What a joke! By the time the real truck has been extricated from the traffic jam and starts calling on the regular stop . . . ha, ha, man, that's the first time they'll even know they've been robbed." He spread wide his arms. "So easy."

DeKok looked serious.

"But you would need accomplices," he objected.

"No problem, I know a couple of guys who'd be happy to help out."

DeKok nodded slowly. He knew a few people like that as well.

"And you figured that all out by yourself?"

"No," denied Karstens, "Maria gave me the idea."

Vledder gaped at the artist and there was disbelief on DeKok's face.

"Maria . . . *your* Maria?"

Karstens nodded cheerfully.

"Oh, yes," he said. "Maria and I have a lot in common. We both like a good glass of wine. We don't need much to live on. My paintings take care of our basic needs. But when the wine supply runs low, Maria goes to work. I think I told you she's an excellent typist and stenographer? Well, she works for a company that supplies part-time personnel. One day she came back with the plan. She had found the complete plan, with all the details in an office file at the company she worked for on a temporary basis. At first she thought it was some sort of security report. But as she read on, it turned out to be a plan to become rich in a hurry."

"And that was just laying around, just like that?"

"More or less."

"What company was that?"

Karstens shrugged nonchalantly.

"The company that owned the truck . . . Houten and Busil Transport Company."

11

"She never worked there."

DeKok was occupied glancing over the reports Vledder had prepared. Some time ago he had asked Vledder to prepare a complete report on everything connected with the case. Since the younger man had all the pertinent information in his computer and had developed a system of his own to correlate that information, it had only been a matter of a few hours before several hundred pages had been dumped on DeKok's desk. He smiled in anticipation of the next time his chief would ask him for a report. He glanced through the pages and noted that Vledder had included all the theories and almost every conversation word for word. Long lists of exhibits and peripheral footnotes were also attached. In a separate envelope were photographs, properly indexed and cross-referenced. Although DeKok had no intention of reading everything, he was filled with silent admiration for the efficiency and thoroughness of his partner.

"Who . . . what?" said DeKok absentmindedly.

Vledder waved his hand in the air.

"Maria . . . Peter Karstens' Maria. I checked. Her full name is Maria Kappelman . . . and according to my information, the temp agency never sent her to Houten and Busil. Karstens is lying. He did not get that famous idea from Maria at all."

DeKok pushed the pile of reports aside. The information amazed him.

"Why did you check?"

Vledder shrugged.

"Just to be sure. I check everything. And you know how the Judge-Advocate always insists on details. Besides, after you asked me for a complete report," he pointed at the stack on DeKok's desk, "I thought it best to include everything I could think of. Also," he continued, "if we want to do anything about Houten and Busil, despite the warning from the Commissaris, it would be a good idea to know for sure if Peter's story is in fact based on truth." He smiled cynically. "Perhaps you have limitless faith in that forger, but not me."

DeKok smiled pleasantly.

"You think he's involved in the robbery, do you?"

Vledder shrugged.

"That . . . eh, I won't say that. Not yet. But in view of the trouble he took . . . the photos, the checking of the routes . . . well, he definitely considered the possibility of those three million most seriously."

DeKok nodded.

"On the basis of that plan."

Vledder pushed his chair back and turned it around. He sat down again and leaned his arms on the backrest of the chair.

"Yes, that convenient plan that was so fortuitously found in the offices of Houten and Busil."

"Where Maria never worked."

Vledder grinned.

"Exactly. You see, something doesn't compute. Peter Karstens just told us a story . . . He purposely directed our attention to the two Directors."

"There is a third possibility."

"A third possibility?"

DeKok nodded calmly.

"Peter Karstens is exactly what I think him to be . . . an honest, spontaneous and straightforward man."

Vledder moved in his chair, becoming increasingly more annoyed.

"Bu . . . but," he muttered, "Maria never . . . has never . . ."

DeKok waved that away as unimportant. He turned half in his chair and motioned toward Inspector Stoops, who had just entered the detective room.

"Mark, you have a moment?"

The cop came closer. His broad smile hidden by an enormous moustache.

"You rang?" he mocked. He looked at Vledder who avoided his glance, a stubborn look on his face. "Do the gentleman have another funeral job to farm out? No problem. I can use the overtime." He plucked the end of his moustache with a sad face. "I'm poor, you know . . . so poor. The mice in our bread box have died of starvation. My wages allow us to live just two weeks per month. The rest of the time, my wife tries to ambush the garbage truck in the hope there is something edible to be found."

DeKok laughed heartily. Stoops was from Utrecht, in the center of Holland and the city was known for its folk humor. With an effort DeKok pulled a serious face.

"A few days ago," he said, "you visited Mrs. Sloten to inform her about the death of her son."

Stoops made a helpless gesture as he pulled up a chair.

"That's more than a week ago."

DeKok nodded.

"Yes, but how did she react?"

"How does a mother react when she hears that her only son has been killed? She was devastated . . . overcome by grief. I was afraid to leave her alone. Afraid she would do herself an injury . . . she was that distressed. Later she calmed down somewhat."

"And then you talked with her?"

Stoops nodded slowly.

"It's hard to find words of comfort in a situation like that. I'm just not good at it. I'm always afraid that I will say the wrong thing . . . may say something hurtful, without realizing it."

DeKok smiled faintly. He felt the same under similar circumstances.

"Did you tell her that it was almost certain that the man who killed her son was the same as his accomplice in the robbery?

"Yes, I did . . . carefully."

"And?"

Stoops stared into the distance, blinked his eyes.

"Now that I think about it . . . it was just as if she already knew. For just a moment I was under the impression she wasn't surprised at all." He paused. "You know, she said something that I remember now. She said: 'Peter . . . Peter won't get away.' There was a peculiar look on her face as she said that."

DeKok glanced at Vledder and noticed that his partner had been busily scribbling in his notebook during the conversation. As DeKok turned back to Stoops, Vledder turned to his keyboard and made some entries.

"Thanks, Mark," said DeKok.

* * *

They drove away from the station house. Vledder, at the wheel of the VW, looked angry and stubborn. He could not understand why DeKok paid so little attention to the fact that Maria had never worked for the transport company. The trust DeKok sometimes placed in people with a criminal past, was often a thorn in Vledder's side. Peter Karstens . . . a notorious forger who imitated the style and techniques of the old masters in a way that brought expert to tears ... a man who looked upon organized society as a personal enemy ... a man like that was trusted by DeKok. Even when Vledder caught him in an outright lie.

He looked at his partner, who peacefully crunched a peppermint, a smile on his face.

"What about what Mrs. Sloten said?" asked Vledder.

"You mean: 'Peter ... Peter won't get away.' That remark?"

"Yes."

DeKok did not answer at once, but dug out another peppermint. Not until he had placed in his mouth and had replaced the roll into one of his pockets, did he speak.

"It looks to me," he said pensively, "as if Mrs. Sloten was not afraid of the killer. On the contrary, she felt she had him in her power."

"How?"

DeKok grimaced.

"If we knew exactly how, we would be a lot closer to the solution. I think that Richard's mother knew all about the robbery. She was thoroughly informed."

Vledder shook his head in despair.

"I can't make head nor tail out of it," he said peevishly. "Stoops makes it clear that Peter Shot killed her son. At the very least one would expect an angry reaction, a feeling of vengeance that would induce her to tell all, I think." He smirked. "But no, she keeps her mouth shut and waits calmly until the killer seeks her out."

DeKok snorted.

"I don't think she figured on that."

Vledder was surprised.

"Then ... what did she figure on?"

"Money . . . lots of money."

"You mean, Richard's part of the loot?"

"Partly."

"But, but," said Vledder, unable to communicate his feelings, "but that's blood money . . . the blood of her own son."

DeKok smiled sadly.

"When there's money involved, especially a lot of money, ethical concepts disappear like snow before the sun. You must disregard all *human* reactions in a case like that. At the time we visited Mrs. Sloten, she did not yet know that her son was dead. That made her silence more understandable. Apparently, as far as she knew, Richard had participated in a successful robbery, a robbery that resulted in a lot of money. Enough money to live a life of luxury . . . something he craved above all things." He paused. "It's harder to understand why she kept silent after she knew her son had been murdered. But I think she wanted to exploit her knowledge."

"Blackmail?"

"Of course, blackmail. I thought about that when Richard's fingerprints were identified. The ease with which the prints were found always seemed a bit suspicious to me."

"Oh?"

"Yes."

"What do you mean?"

"I mean that Richard could have left those fingerprints in the car on purpose."

"Really?"

"We certainly cannot ignore that possibility. I said something early on during this case. Richard could possibly get off with a light sentence and then he, and his mother, would have some powerful leverage on his accomplice . . . and the loot."

Vledder grinned suddenly.

"And that means that Richard betrayed his accomplice even before the robbery."

DeKok rummaged in the glove department and located a forgotten candy bar. With a satisfied look he unwrapped it and took a bite.

"It wouldn't be the first time," he said, his mouth full of chocolate. "I can give you a number of examples of that. Richard Sloten *could* have, right after the robbery . . . *and* after he had made sure that his part of the haul was safely stashed away, reported himself to the police with an acceptable story. But then his 'treason' would have been too obvious. Leaving his fingerprints behind was much subtler and much more difficult to figure out."

"But that also means that you're prepared to accept that Richard all along was planning to lay his hands on the total haul, on all the money."

DeKok nodded with emphasis, swallowing the last of his chocolate.

"It was his nature . . . cunning, but without a taste for violence. I think his mother knew all about the plan and that she decided, after Richard was killed, to complete the plan . . . slightly adapted to the new circumstances."

"What new circumstances?"

"The original plan, after all, did not include the possibility of Richard being killed."

They drove on in silence. Vledder was no longer angry. He thought about the death of Richard's mother and the new theories DeKok had advanced. Then he brought up a subject that had bothered him for some time.

"What about Monika Buwalda?" he asked.

DeKok evaded the question.

"I've been meaning to talk to you about her," he said paternally.

"What?"

"Yes, I was very much aware how you appeared to be besotted by her. You hardly dared look at her."

"Well . . ."

"And after she fainted, your hands shook as you put her to bed. She's very beautiful, but you were a bit too much influenced by her, I think."

"Well . . ."

"Please, I don't mean to lecture you, but although you asked all the right questions, I'm not sure you heard any of the answers."

Vledder regained a little of his composure.

"No problem there," he said, "I was recording."

"What!?" It was DeKok's turn to be surprised.

"Yes," admitted Vledder sheepishly, "I've been carrying a little pocket recorder for some time." He put a hand to his breast pocket and pulled out a small tape recorder. DeKok looked at the instrument with disapproval.

"So, now you're resorting to electronic information gathering, or whatever they call it."

"Data gathering."

"Never mind, how long have you been doing that?"

"A few weeks."

"You use it all the time?"

"No, only when I want to be sure my notes are correct."

"Good, don't let it ever take the place of your eyes and ears. A machine can never replace those."

"Yes, well . . ."

"As in the case of Monika. If you had not been relying on that . . . that *thing* there, you would not have been hypnotized."

"Hypnotized!" protested Vledder.

"Yes, hypnotized. I don't exactly know what it is with that woman, but there is something unwholesome about her."

"She's gorgeous."

"Ah, yes, but remember, beauty is only skin deep."

"Rather trite."

"Maybe." DeKok shook his head. "No," he went on, "if you want to see a truly beautiful woman, take a look at Maria, Peter Karstens' friend."

"What! She flaunts herself."

"So does Monika, my young friend. But with Monika there is a purpose to what she does, she uses her body to gain something. Maria . . . Maria," smiled DeKok, "is just as free with showing her body and just as proud of it . . . but she doesn't use it as a weapon. She enjoys your enjoyment." He paused. "Maria is a *generous* person," he concluded.

"Now, see here, DeKok," began Vledder.

"Never mind," interrupted DeKok. "I should probably not have said anything. But think about it this way . . . you could explain Maria to Celine . . . but how would you explain Monika to your fiancee?"

When Vledder did think about it that way, he had the grace to blush. Celine, his fiancee, was a flight attendant for KLM and was often away on intercontinental routes.

"All right, DeKok, you win," said Vledder after a long pause. Then another thought struck him. "But I still don't understand something about Mrs. Sloten," he said in a different tone of voice. "She was playing with fire. After all, she knew that Richard's accomplice didn't shrink back from anything. She *must* have know Peter Shot's reputation."

DeKok smiled inwardly at the adroit way in which Vledder changed the subject.

"We don't know what she thought," he said seriously. "Perhaps she had some idea about private justice."

"How do you mean?"

"That she wanted to punish the killer of her son in her own way . . . that she had little faith in the type of justice handed down by our courts. Maybe that's why she kept silent. Of course," he admitted, "it's all highly speculative. We can't ask her anymore." He rubbed the back of his neck. "We lost that opportunity."

"Still . . ."

"Yes, still, as you say. Blackmailers, as a rule, are very careful people. They well know the dangers to which they expose themselves. That's why they work on safeguards . . . securities."

"What sort of safeguards?"

DeKok shrugged.

They usually have a safe place where they keep the items that form the basis of their blackmail. Photos, films, documents and such are usually . . ." He stopped suddenly and slapped his forehead. "The doll . . . of course . . . the doll."

"Of course," agreed Vledder suddenly.

"That's where she kept it," said DeKok.

12

They drove through a narrow street with similar, monotonous houses. DeKok looked around.

"It's here?"

Vledder discovered a parking space, barely enough for the diminutive VW. He backed into the spot.

"Bestevaar Street," he nodded. He switched off the engine and searched in a breast pocket. His hand emerged with a wrinkled piece of paper with the number 753 written on it."

Reluctantly they left the car and walked slowly along the pavement toward the indicated number. DeKok stopped to observe a group of children playing. Apart from the group, leaning against the front of one of the row houses was a small boy, about seven, or eight. The gray sleuth recognized him as the boy from the chapel at Muller's funeral. Among the playing children he discovered the two little, blonde girls. He walked toward the boy and waved at the children.

"Are you keeping an eye on your little sisters?"

The boy gave him a suspicious look. His sharp eyes absorbed the features of the old cop.

"I don't know you."

DeKok smiled.

"Is your mother home?"

"Mother is always home. I run the errands and do the shopping."

DeKok pointed at the children who were bouncing an old tennis ball against a blank wall.

"Don't you want to play, too?"

The little boy shook his head calmly and then nodded in the direction of the two little girls with an understanding beyond his years.

"They never watch where they're going," he said sadly. "They cross the street without looking left or right. The other day one of 'em almost got under a car. You can't let them out of your sight, ever."

DeKok placed a hand in the narrow shoulder and squeezed slightly.

"I know just how you feel," he said, sympathy in his voice. "I had two younger sisters as well." He turned away but after a few steps he turned back. "If, eh, if Mr. Houten happens to be at your house, we'll come back some other time."

The boy looked startled and his face turned red.

"Mr. Houten don't come here no more. Never again. My mother doesn't want to ever see him again."

DeKok nodded his understanding. Again he turned away into the direction of number 753. His young partner looked at him askance.

"Do you think that was a responsible thing to do? I mean, ethically? To approach that kid like that?"

DeKok compressed his lips, took a deep breath and then he spat: "You talk about ethics? What about three murders?"

Vledder reacted like a chastised child and abandoned the touchy subject.

They stopped in front of number 753. DeKok looked at a plain plastic nameplate with *M. Muller* in white letters on a black background. He pressed the knob next to the name. Somewhere inside a gong bonged.

After a few minutes a young, blonde woman opened the door. For the first time DeKok saw her face, without the veil she had worn at the funeral. Peter Doon was right. Ria Muller was a beautiful woman. Class, as Peter had said . . . certainly worth a second look. DeKok did. The dark dress accentuated in a delicious way the delightful curves and the long, gold-blonde hair gleamed exhilaratingly in the dark corridor. For a moment she took his breath away.

Ria Muller looked surprised at the two men on her doorstep.

DeKok again became totally professional. With a courteous bow he removed his hat and introduced himself.

"My name is DeKok . . . with kay-oh-kay," he said politely. He waved at Vledder. "My colleague, Vledder. We're Police Inspectors."

There was suspicion and fear in her startlingly blue eyes. "Detectives?"

DeKok nodded, keeping his hat in front of his chest.

"We, eh, we would like to talk to you," he said with hesitation in his voice. "We would have liked to talk to you sooner, but we felt you were entitled to some privacy . . . I mean . . . you needed some time to recover from the shock of your husband's sudden death. At least . . . to get over the first, immense grief as far as that is possible. Of course, the sorrow will always be there, but we know how devastating the first few days can be." He smiled a fatherly smile. "But we really can't wait much longer."

A faint smile appeared around her full, sensuous lips.

"That, that was very considerate of you." She stepped aside. "Why don't you come in."

The two cops entered the house. She closed the front door behind them and then led the way towards a spacious room, dominated by an expensive leather-and-walnut couch set. She made an inviting gesture.

"Please sit down."

DeKok unbuttoned his old raincoat and looked around. Apart from the truly imposing couches and easy chairs, the room contained few luxuries. The buffet against the wall was of average quality and showed clear signs of disrepair. He lowered himself onto the couch and placed his hat on the floor next to him.

"Much to our regret," he began, "we have to admit that our research so far has not been very successful. For some time now, we have been after a suspect, Peter Shot by name, but he has so far eluded us." He looked at her. "Have you ever heard the name before?"

Mrs. Muller shook her head. She frowned.

"Is he the one who . . . did he . . . my husband?"

She was unable to complete the question. DeKok nodded slowly.

"We do not have absolute proof, but there are certain indications that seem to confirm that Peter Shot is responsible for the death of at least three people . . . your husband, Richard Sloten and Richard's mother." He gave her another sharp look. "Did you know Richard Sloten?"

She returned his look with suspicion.

"Should I?"

DeKok gave her a winning smile.

"No, no, not at all. However, during our investigation certain questions came up . . . important questions. For instance, how come the robbers were so well informed?"

She nodded her understanding.

"You're looking for an informer."

"And a motive."

"For what?"

DeKok's face was expressionless.

"The murder of your husband."

She plucked at the collar of her dress.

"It . . . it *was* murder?"

DeKok did not answer. He gave her a searching look, read the unrest in her eyes. After a while he leaned toward her.

"How well did you know your husband? I mean, was he always open with you . . . did he talk about his work . . . his problems?"

Red spots appeared on her throat.

"Martin and I had a good marriage."

It was said in a challenging and acrimonious tone.

DeKok nodded calmly.

"But even in the best marriages the spouses are not always completely open with each other," he said seriously. "That does not necessarily mean that the relationship is in any way harmed, or damaged."

She cocked her head at him.

"You think my husband kept secrets from me?"

"Yes."

"Such as?"

Again she reacted sharply. After the question she pressed her lips together and gave him an angry look.

"Maybe he was afraid of losing you."

"There was no reason for him to fear that," she said vehemently, almost defensively.

DeKok looked at her with cold eyes.

"So you knew about his fear?"

Suddenly she stood up, a wild look in her eyes.

"No," she screamed. "I never once, ever, believed that Martin didn't trust me." She lowered her voice. "But I knew what

121

was being said . . . the gossip. I have heard those things, but there were no grounds." She sighed deeply as she sat back down. "It was a party at the Company last year . . . in November. The Company was celebrating so many years of being in business. There was a band and there was dancing. That night Mr. Houten showed more than the usual amount of interest in me. It was noticeable. Mr. Houten is all right, but he is not exactly the type of man for whom I could feel anything. He's too much the man of the world, too . . . too smooth." She made a helpless gesture. "And what could I do? He was Martin's boss. I danced with him . . . several times. Later the personnel talked about it, especially the women. I think it was mostly jealousy."

"And Martin heard that kind of talk?"

"Yes," she said, "he must have."

"Did you ever discuss it with him?"

"No."

DeKok shook his head.

"But isn't it because of that . . . the gossip, that Martin wanted to quit driving the long hauls?"

She shrugged.

"Martin only said that he was tired of those long trips. He wanted to transfer to the money transports. That way he could be home every day. It was better for the children, too."

"So he asked for a transfer?"

She shook her head.

"No Martin didn't. I did."

DeKok raised his eyebrows, but the usual gymnastics did not manifest themselves.

"*You* went to ask if Martin could transfer?" he asked, surprise in his voice.

She wrung her hands.

"Martin said: you go to the office, put on something nice. If you ask Houten, he won't refuse."

"And?"

"Mr. Houten had no objections. 'I'll take care of it,' he said."

DeKok rubbed his forehead, as if in pain. Meanwhile his brain was in turmoil. He glanced at Ria surreptitiously. There was no question that the answers of the young woman had surprised him. Apparently Martin had taken the gossip about his wife with a considerable grain of salt. The gossip had certainly not bothered him. On the contrary, he seemed to have used the interest shown in his wife by Mr. Houten as a lever to get a transfer within the company. Because of his marriage ... because of the children?

"What did Peter Doon think about the fact that Martin had stopped doing long trips?"

Mrs. Muller smiled.

"Peter thought it to be a terrible mistake. He and Martin got along so well together. But Peter is a confirmed bachelor and ridiculed any attempts at tying him down to a wife and family. That's why he doesn't mind the long trips. He likes them. It makes no never mind to him whether he's away from home for a long time, or not." She grinned wanly. "A girl in every port, or, in this case, in every town. That's Peter."

DeKok pulled his lower lip and let it plop back.

"Did you ever discuss the possibility of a robbery, I mean, an attack on the money transports?"

"Never."

"Not even as a joke?"

"No."

"You mean, Martin wasn't afraid? After all, in the end he became the victim of such an attack."

Ria Muller shook her head.

"He never," she said, hesitating over the words, "he never talked about it."

123

DeKok looked at her.

"And you . . . were you ever afraid that something would happen to him?"

She made a sad gesture.

"Every job has its own risks. The long-distance trips weren't without danger either."

DeKok leaned back against the high back of the couch. All his experience and knowledge seemed to be inadequate at this time. He could not shake the feeling that Ria Muller had built a wall around herself, an impenetrable wall to protect her against the outside world. It was if she already knew the questions and had prepared the answers.

"Did Martin ever want to be rich?"

The question sounded banal, even as he spoke it.

But Ria gave him another wan smile. With a hand she rubbed the expensive material of the chair in which she was seated.

"This furniture is one of my whims . . . a dream . . . a concrete illusion. Although it was really above our budget, Martin did not object." She paused. "I still have eight payments left. Martin never made a lot of money and he had to work hard for what he got. The children are also not cheap. Martin sometimes used to say something like: and to think that every day, behind the cabin of my truck, there's all the money in the world."

She paused again. Her hands rested in her lap and she stared in front of her. Then she turned her head and she vaguely seemed to observe the old Inspector, but her mind was elsewhere. An almost imperceptible smile played around the finely carved lips. It was as if her face resisted the attempt to be cheered in any way. After a while she suddenly stood up.

"I'll make you some coffee." The tone did not allow any disagreement. She went to the kitchen.

DeKok looked after her as she left the room. He had met so many beautiful women in his long career and it always seemed to him that their beauty was on a par with the amount of trouble they were in. As if suffering was the price to pay for beauty. One way or the other the women looked alike . . . had a magical effect on his soul, so receptive to feminine charms.

Ria returned from the kitchen and placed a tray with cups, saucers, sugar and cream on the low cocktail table. DeKok watched her in silence. When she had filled the cups, he asked a question, almost carelessly.

"Do you know why Martin deviated from his route, that morning?"

She looked down on him. All color drained from her face.

"Who says so?" she asked breathlessly.

"Mr. Houten . . . among others."

Suddenly she lost all self-control. Her poise melted away like snow before the sun. She shook her head violently and her golden hair danced around her head.

"It isn't true," she cried out. Her voice was angry, shrieking. "It isn't true," she repeated. Martin did *not* go a different route. They're lies . . . all lies." She placed her feet wider apart and pulled back her head. She glared at DeKok, nostrils wide and breathing hard. "I know what they want to do. I know it. They want to besmirch my husband's name after his death, when he can't defend himself." She stretched out an arm with an accusing finger pointed at DeKok. "And you . . . you play their game. Martin had *nothing* to do with that robbery." She took a deep breath, calmed down a bit. "I was married to a man who was as honest as the day is long." She paused and nodded to herself. "An honest man . . . you hear . . . a man who would never get involved in anything underhanded."

With short, decisive steps she walked toward the door and opened it wide.

"And now I want you to leave . . . at once."

DeKok sighed, stood up and gave a last, rueful look at the inviting cups of coffee. He motioned toward Vledder. She walked down the corridor with them and opened the front door. Then DeKok turned toward her.

"I do hope," he said seriously, "that I will never have to disappoint you."

13

Vledder smirked.

"And so the great detective is chased away, like a dog with its tail between its legs."

He sounded cheerful.

DeKok just shrugged.

"It's her house," he said. His voice was resigned. "And who can blame a woman who wants to keep the memory of her husband pure, even idealistic . . . if she wants to forget, or obscure the fact that there may have been something unsavory about his death . . . if she wants to deny to herself that his death is connected to a crime . . . that he was . . ." He broke off. "I can understand that," he added, after a brief pause. He smiled. "It's too bad about the coffee. The aroma made my mouth water."

They reached the car and climbed in. Vledder extricated the vehicle from the narrow streets and drove into the direction of town. After a while he broke the silence.

"So you really think that Martin Muller has nothing to do with it?"

DeKok seemed to ignore the question and stared morosely through the windshield.

"Well?" urged Vledder.

"You know, Dick," DeKok said finally, "there are just too many connections in this case. There are so many correlations that I sometimes feel that *everybody* is connected to this particular robbery . . . that everyone knew about it. But no matter which threads you follow, no matter what connections you may see . . . whatever combinations of people are involved, there has to be a unique combination somewhere. Somehow there has to be a connection between Peter Shot, mother Sloten and her son Richard. It's extremely frustrating that we seem to be unable to find *those* particular threads."

He paused. The image of an angry Ria Muller was clear in front of his eyes. From his slouched position he looked up at Vledder.

"Did you ever take a look at the official route they were supposed to take?"

Vledder shook his head, frowning at a reckless bicyclist who was intent on passing the VW. The car might be old and decrepit, thought Vledder, but at least it is still capable of outrunning a bicycle.

"No," he said. "Frankly, I never even asked for it. There has to be a route map, of course. I think we'll be able to find one in the office of Busil & Houten. Somewhere they must keep a record of the different routes they follow."

DeKok grinned.

"There are a lot of things written down in the offices of Busil and Houten."

Vledder nodded agreement at the rear-view mirror, where he saw the cyclist disappear in the distance.

"For instance," he said thoughtfully, "how to make a couple of millions in a few easy steps." He paused as if for emphasis. "That begs the question, of course, how that plan happened to wind up with your friend Karstens."

DeKok ignored the implied question. It was not certain if he had even heard it. He stared ahead. There was a determined look on his face. His voice was grim when he spoke.

"It's about time that we start ignoring the prohibition of the Judge-Advocate and that we pay a visit to the remarkable duo of Busil and Houten."

"Now?"

DeKok shook his head.

"It's still too much day ... besides, I don't want you involved."

Vledder frowned.

"Which means," he said slowly, "that whatever you're planning cannot stand the light of day."

DeKok merely smiled, a faint movement of lips.

"Sometimes, Dick ... sometimes you make such intelligent remarks. It almost frightens me."

Vledder's face fell.

"No need to be sarcastic," he grumbled.

"I'm sorry," answered DeKok. He sounded sincerely contrite. "I was only thinking of your welfare."

Vledder's face became red. With an abrupt movement he steered the car toward the curb and parked. He switched off the engine. DeKok looked at him in surprise.

"What's the matter with you?"

Vledder's face was red. His lips were pressed together and his eyes were angry. He adjusted the seat and turned toward his old partner.

"Now you listen to me, Detective-Inspector DeKok," he said with a quiver in his voice. "I'm tired of you protecting me. By now I'm old enough and wise enough to know what I want and what I don't want ... what I will do and what I won't do." He paused and took a deep breath. Somewhat calmer, he continued: "We handle this case together ... as *equal* partners. I am getting tired of looking like a fool when you suddenly conjure the solution out of thin air, like a magician who suddenly pulls a rabbit out of a hat."

He placed his hands on the steering wheel and was now completely under control. But there was still a hard tone to his words as he concluded.

"I want to be *part* of this investigation. In everything, you understand?"

DeKok looked at him with a twinkle in his eyes.

"Is that all?"

"That's it."

"Part of *every* thing?" asked DeKok.

"*Every* thing," agreed Vledder with emphasis.

"Even when I take idiotic risks?"

"Especially when you take idiotic risks."

DeKok made a resigned gesture. His hand strayed to his vest pocket and emerged with a piece of licorice. He looked at it, dusted it off and placed it in his mouth. He chewed contentedly for a few seconds.

"All right," he said finally, "tonight I'll do some breaking and entering."

Vledder did not seem surprised.

"Where?" he asked evenly.

"At the offices of Busil & Houten."

* * *

Vledder parked the VW in a nearly deserted parking lot. The engine continued dieseling for a while after he turned the key. He started it up again and this time kept the car in gear as he turned the key. That did the trick; with a last, complaining splutter, the engine shut off. It was a measure of his distraction that he did not remark on the vagaries of the ancient vehicle. He pulled up his sleeve and looked at his watch. It was almost two o'clock in the morning. The young Inspector glanced at DeKok who made no move to get out of the car.

"This spot OK?" he asked.

DeKok nodded.

"Just don't lock the doors when you get out," said the old Inspector gruffly. It was a measure of his distraction that he did not comment on the use of "OK," an expression he usually detested. "If we have to depart in a hurry, we'll have no time to lose at all, at all." He searched his pockets. Vledder watched as he unearthed a few pieces of cloth, some large paper clips and a toffee. DeKok handed the cloths and the paper clips to Vledder and placed the toffee in his mouth.

"Hang this over the license tags," he instructed. "It might be thought a bit messy if it came out that a police vehicle was connected to a burglary."

Vledder grinned boyishly. He was getting caught up in the adventure. He pointed through the windshield at an illuminated area behind a high fence. Within the enclosure they saw a large number of bright red tractor-trailers and double truck-trailer combinations. All vehicles showed the "Houten & Busil" legend in large, white letters.

"Tell me, what do you think you'll find in there?"

DeKok made a nonchalant gesture.

"I don't know exactly. It's just a feeling. I mean ... I haven't really thought it through." He nodded in the direction of the office building. "I just feel that there should be enough information inside that building to allow us to ask some further questions of Houten and his partner, Busil ... with, or without, the permission of the Judge-Advocate."

He snorted. Vledder looked faintly amused.

"And you're going to find it," suggested Vledder.

"Yes," said DeKok, disapproval in his voice. "The restrictions of the Judge-Advocate drive me to distraction. Since when is Houten above the Law? Is anybody? Why shouldn't we approach him and what makes him so special? Why this ridiculous concern?" He sighed deeply. "Sometimes," he added sadly, "I have the distinct feeling that the so-called Palace of Justice is rapidly becoming overcrowded with people who are actually *afraid* to take steps against the ever increasing, encroaching wave of criminality."

Vledder gaped.

"Really? What makes you think that?"

"Oh, a lot of little things all put together. The careful, almost timid way in which they act against known criminals. The way they seem to go deliberately out of their way to make it easier for the criminal to hide, or continue his ongoing, illegal operations. The elastic tolerance of the civilian lawmakers . . . the almost pathetic attempt at interference with various investigations . . . the way the Government seems bent on denying the Police even the most elementary crime fighting ability."

"Surely, you don't mean that," protested Vledder.

"Well," admitted DeKok, "perhaps not entirely. But," he continued more vigorously, "it is a fact that the application of the Law is lax and that the sentencing procedures are far too lenient in many cases. And," he raised a finger in the air, "there seems to be more concern for the rights of the criminals, than for those of the victims."

"You make it sound very sad."

"But it *is* sad," said DeKok with some emphasis. "The lawless elements seem to get the upper hand. Not just here," he said, shaking his head, "but everywhere. You told me how there are at least 500 police officers killed in the line of duty in the States. In England more and more police officers are now carrying firearms, How long before the Bobby of yesterday will be patrolling in riot gear with a submachine gun?"

Vledder looked worried.

"But you still believe in Justice, don't you?" he asked anxiously.

The gray sleuth looked at his partner. A genuine smile spread over his face.

"Like I do in our Dear Lord," he said cheerfully, stepping out of the car. "And as far as I know, He has not yet eliminated *Thou shalt not kill* from the Ten Commandments."

Vledder, too, left the car. With a smile he attached the cloths to the license plates. Then, side by side, they walked toward the gate.

DeKok felt the tiredness leave him. There were periods, too often and too close together, when he felt his task was insurmountable. Then he was tempted to chuck it all and retire. But there were also invigorating times, when he still felt the blood racing through his system and when he felt ready for any challenge. He admitted to himself that these occasions were more frequent since Vledder had become his regular partner.

And this was such a moment

DeKok stopped in front of the iron gates, topped by hostile looking pointed shafts. From his pockets he produced a small, brass cylinder, a present from a former burglar. He guarded Henkie's present as a rare and valuable gift. It enabled him to open just about any lock ever made. He hoped he always used it in the furtherance of his pursuit for Justice. It took only thirty seconds, or less, when DeKok pushed open the heavy door.

"Is the gate always locked at night?" asked Vledder.

DeKok nodded.

"Every driver has a key. The long-distance trips are timed to arrive during the day and if a local driver gets back late, he can always open the gate and park his vehicle inside."

"Strange they don't operate around the clock."

"As I understand it, they run two shifts only. That's for the yard, you understand. The office normally operates from nine to five."

They passed through the gate and slowly and soundlessly pushed it shut behind them.

"That was a simple lock," remarked DeKok. "The office may give us a little more trouble."

Staying in the shadows of the trucks they crept forward. After about a hundred yards they reached the office building. It was a relatively low structure with just two floors. The lower windows were secured with shutters.

DeKok took a long look at the lock in the front door. Then he adjusted something on the small instrument in his hands and a slender probe entered the lock. Slowly he moved the probe around inside the lock. Then he froze and withdrew the instrument.

"Easy, after all?" suggested Vledder.

DeKok shook his head.

"It isn't locked," whispered DeKok hoarsely.

Then he pointed at some fresh marks on the wood of the door frame. He had not noticed them at first.

"Broken into," he whispered, tension in his voice.

Vledder reached for his pistol.

"You want to call for back-up?"

DeKok shook his head.

"That takes too long," he answered softly. "Besides," he added with a sly grin, "how would we explain our presence here?" He looked around, evaluating the situation. "Stay here," he commanded. "Wait two minutes and then go in . . . carefully."

"Where will you be?"

"There is another door in the back. I don't think I'll need more than a minute to get through. Add maybe a minute for going around the building and we should enter just about simultaneously."

He took Vledder by the shoulder and shook it slightly.

"Behind this door is a hallway with stairs. The private offices are upstairs, to the right, almost in the center. Behind the private offices is a rather large room which contains, among other things, the safe."

Vledder frowned in the dark.

"How come you're so well informed?"

"I have been here once before. You'll remember, in connection with the B&G case, for background. Odd," he added, that also involved an armored truck . . . different firm, though."*

Vledder shrugged off the explanation. If DeKok had been here once before, the lay-out of the office would be as he said. It was generally believed that DeKok had a photographic memory.

DeKok tapped Vledder on the shoulder.

"Start counting from now."

With that he disappeared into the shadows.

The young Inspector watched the lighted dial of his watch and smiled. Typical DeKok remark, he mused. Wanted him to count as if watches with lighted dials had not been invented. Meanwhile he double checked the readiness of his pistol. DeKok was not armed, he knew. DeKok did not believe in brute force. Vledder considered it his duty and privilege to back up the old man with more persuasive measures, if necessary. It was seldom, if ever, necessary.

When the required time had elapsed, Vledder pushed open the door. As DeKok had predicted, there was the hallway. It was larger than he expected. He saw a white, marble bust on a wooden pedestal and behind it the stairs. He took the pistol in his

---

* See: DeKok and the Sorrowing Tomcat.

hand and slowly walked up the stairs, staying near the edges of the broad, wooden steps. He waited at the top of the stairs and listened. There was no sound, no matter how hard he strained to hear. It was an absolute silence . . . strange, unreal, threatening . . . as if the whole world was holding its collective breath.

He looked down the corridor which stretched out before him. It was a wide corridor with frosted glass on either side. Yet it was darker than downstairs. When his eyes became accustomed to the diminished light, he saw a low figure at the end of the corridor, Big and massive, yet giving the impression of incredible age. An almost tender smile fled across his face. He recognized DeKok who slinked near on hands and feet, staying below the feeble light that came through the frosted windows. DeKok was not taking any chances at throwing shadows. Vledder dropped down as well. They met each other in the middle of the corridor.

The old sleuth pointed a thumb at a wide, mahogany door. They waited a brief moment, then both stood up. With a sudden, powerful movement DeKok kicked open the door. Vledder ran inside, the pistol in his hand leading the way. In about the center of the room stood a tall, athletically built man. His silhouette was clearly visible against the light from outside.   Startled, the man turned.

DeKok aimed a flashlight at his face.

Vledder's mouth fell open.

"That's . . . that is . . ."

DeKok nodded.

"Peter . . . Peter Doon."

136

14

Slowly, hesitatingly, Peter Doon raised his hands in the air. He laughed sheepishly, like a child caught doing something naughty. But his eyes were alert.

DeKok switched off the flashlight and leaned against the door. Vledder waved his weapon and directed Doon away from the center of the room. He ordered him to place his hands against the wall and spread his legs. Then Vledder frisked him quickly and efficiently. He found no weapon and replaced his own pistol in the shoulder holster.

"You want me to cuff him?" asked Vledder of DeKok.

DeKok shook his head.

"No, it's such an unnecessary indignity."

Vledder allowed Doon to turn around.

"Isn't that so, Mr. Doon?" asked DeKok.

"What?"

"Don't you think handcuffs are an unnecessary indignity. A wanton abuse of power, an unwarranted deprivation of one's freedom?"

The young man smiled. It gave his handsome face an added depth. Then he searched DeKok's face and found no irony there.

"You're right," admitted Doon. "But," he continued, gesturing at Vledder, "a cannon like that is just as inhibitive. You never know. What if the pistol carrier gets nervous?"

Vledder grinned broadly, patting his shoulder holster.

"Don't worry," he said pleasantly, "I only get nervous when the weapon is in someone else's hands."

DeKok moved away from the door.

"What are you looking for, here?"

"Money."

"From your own boss?"

Peter Doon shook his head.

"He isn't my boss anymore. I quit, right after the robbery. I can't work for these crooks any longer."

DeKok cocked his head, a look of surprise on his face.

"Crooks? The firm has a very good name."

Doon grinned savagely.

"I thought about it a long time . . . that robbery where Martin was killed. There's only *one* person who could have had a hand in it."

"Who?"

"Houten."

DeKok's expression of surprise changed to utter astonishment.

"But what could he have to gain by killing his own employees?"

Doon shook his head as if to clear the cobwebs from his mind. He looked at DeKok.

"You never worked here. You don't know them. You don't know them the way I do. I have been here a few years, you know. Houten fancies Ria, I told you that before. His own wife is no sweetheart. She lives in the country in a large house and has a hole in her hand that you wouldn't believe. She never has enough money. And he, himself, is not much better when it comes to spending. Every night on the nightclub circuit and he has a real penchant for fast, expensive cars. What do you figure that costs?"

"A lot of money."

Doon gestured agreement.

"Exactly . . . lots of money and if you put two and two together, he has an excellent motive for murder. Martin gone, Ria available and a lot of extra, tax free cash . . . you know what I mean?"

DeKok gave a meaningful look around the office.

"And you think the money is here?"

Doon shrugged his shoulders.

"Perhaps not all of it . . . just part of it. After all, he has to stow it somewhere, right?"

DeKok nodded thoughtfully.

"We went to Ria's," he said slowly. "Perhaps I am wrong, but I was under the distinct impression that she was not exactly happy with Houten's attention."

Peter Doon gave him a pitying smile.

"Ach, sir, Ria doesn't want to let on. She makes the effort because of her boy, the eight year old. A sensitive little tyke who loved Martin . . . his father, very much. You see, she doesn't want to upset the boy by being too public about her feelings for Houten." He paused and looked around. "How did you know I was here?"

DeKok shrugged.

"We just happened to be passing."

Doon grinned knowingly.

"Sure and if you believe that, I have a good deal for you on the Brooklyn bridge. Come now, the famous Detective-Inspector DeKok doesn't go around playing burglar at night." He narrowed his eyes. "You *knew* I would be here."

The gray sleuth gave him a searching look.

"Who could have told us?"

Doon blinked his eyes.

"That I don't know. I told nobody what I was planning to do. It was just a spontaneous thought this evening. I was thinking about the robbery ... and about Martin ... and about the money."

DeKok nodded his understanding.

"So you decided to risk it."

It was Peter Doon's turn to shrug.

"I didn't think there was a lot of risk involved. I still have a key to the gate. I could come in and lock it behind me." He paused to look sharply at DeKok. "That's why I don't believe you just happened to be passing. There was no way you could have seen that somebody was inside."

DeKok smiled mysteriously. He turned around and walked toward the door. Then he opened it wide.

"You may go."

Doon gave him a suspicious look.

"Just like that?"

"Just like that," confirmed DeKok. "You're free to go. We did not see you here ... did not talk to you."

"And if they pick me up later?"

"Then you keep your mouth shut."

Doon became even more suspicious.

"And if I don't?"

DeKok grinned mischievously.

"It'll be two against one. We will stoutly maintain that you must have suffered hallucinations and we know nothing."

* * *

Vledder pulled the cloths off the license plates, seated himself behind the wheel and started the car. As he pulled away he looked once more at the gate that gave access to the large parking lot within the fence. DeKok had locked it securely. The old man was slouched in the passenger seat, a satisfied look on his face.

Vledder pointed a thumb at the gate.

"What are we going to do with *this* burglary?"

"Nothing. They'll probably figure out in the morning that there has been a break-in and they'll call the police."

"Yes, and one of our colleagues will get the call." Vledder shook his head in frustration. "And he will start an investigation."

"Exactly."

"And we know the perpetrator."

DeKok seemed amused.

"We do?" he asked innocently.

Vledder gave him a quick glance.

"Why did you let him go?"

DeKok smiled. He recalled the suspicious look on Doon's face. He also remembered the triumphant look that replaced it when he realized that Vledder and DeKok could never admit having seen him. Doon was wrong, but he did not know that.

"Why bother to arrest a burglar who, as far as we know, stole nothing. Is that going to help us in this case? We're hunting several million *and* a triple murderer." He paused to place a peppermint in his mouth. "And you'll admit that our being there could, to say the least, raise a few awkward questions. Doon figured that out, although for the wrong reasons. But the fact that he thought about it all, gives me pause. He's not dumb, is Peter Doon. That's also why I left immediately . . . without completing our own investigation in the private offices of Houten & Busil."

Vledder looked thoughtful.

"I don't understand that," he finally admitted.

DeKok pushed himself into a more upright position.

"Park here somewhere and please turn off the engine and switch off the lights."

"But why?"

DeKok rubbed the tip of his nose.

"If I am right, the police will be here in a few minutes."

Vledder slowed down and parked the car, half hidden by some bushes that grew close to the road. He opened the window on the driver's side. Apart from the constant background noise of insects and other small animals in the park, there was absolute silence. Suddenly there was the sound of sirens. It approached rapidly and soon they saw the reflection of rotating blue and red lights. Vledder looked at DeKok.

"He called the police." Vledder had a tendency to state the obvious.

DeKok nodded complacently.

"Probably from the nearest phone booth . . . anonymously, of course. If we had stayed behind we might have been arrested by our own colleagues . . . certainly they would have surprised us."

Vledder released his breath in a long sigh. His face was pale.

"We would have had a lot of trouble explaining ourselves," he said softly.

DeKok nodded. Vledder could hear the crunching of the peppermint DeKok was chewing.

"Doon realized that, of course. I saw it in his eyes as he left."

The sirens fell silent. The light continued as two police cars approached rapidly from the direction of the city. DeKok and Vledder bent down, below the level of the dashboard. The unmarked vehicle looked like just one more decrepit VW parked along the road. The police cars ignored them. A little later they heard the screeching of brakes and the sound of doors slamming.

142

"Sorry, my friends," joked DeKok. "Another wild goose chase, I'm afraid. You're too late. The gate is closed and the birds have flown . . . mustard after the meal . . . the barn has burned and the horse is dead . . . no need to cover the well, the calf has drowned . . . many have been called, but . . ."

Vledder interrupted him. Sometimes DeKok could carry on with one obscure quotation after another. Before they became too excruciating, it was always best to cut him off, if possible.

"Now what?" asked Vledder as he started the engine.

"Back to the office . . . let's find out if they have discovered anything new and then . . . to bed." He looked at his watch. "It's almost three o'clock."

They drove on in silence. The inner city of Amsterdam was still wide awake. Vague figures moved in the shadows and taxis seemed to be everywhere. Neon lights flickered on and off. A young prostitute screamed at a man who sauntered away, hands in his pockets and a guilty look on his face. DeKok watched resignedly, not missing anything, but watching as with another part of his mind. He knew the city at every hour of the day, or night. He knew its evils and its goodness. The lights might change, the sounds might be different, the atmosphere was never the same, but the background that was Amsterdam was always there.

He tapped Vledder lightly on the arm.

"Check the register tomorrow and find out what has been reported regarding the burglary at Houten & Busil. They will probably have responded from Louis Dijssel Street station. I do especially want to know if anything has been reported missing."

"Would that be the case?" asked Vledder, startled.

"Well," said DeKok, shrugging, "we don't really know how long Doon was in the office before we got there."

"You think he was really looking for money?"

DeKok pursed his lips.

"Mm . . .," he grunted, "I don't know, but it does seem logical. That is," he added, "if you accept his reasoning. Mind you," he went on, "I can't quite rid myself of the same theory either. Somehow I feel that the firm is involved. But," he concluded, resolutely, "it is ridiculous to presume that Houten would be so stupid as to hide all, or part, of the money in his own office."

Vledder slowed down and looked at the young prostitute who was now pursuing the man that had just left her.

"Stupid pimp," she yelled, "half baked mackerel!"

"Mackerel?" wondered Vledder aloud.

"Sure," said DeKok. "The French word for pimp is *maquereau* or . . . mackerel."

"I don't know what the Quarter is coming to," sighed Vledder. "Pimps slink away with their tails between their legs and whores make allusions to foreign languages."

DeKok smiled tolerantly.

Vledder speeded up and soon parked the old car behind the station. They walked around the building to enter by the front entrance.

As they entered the station, the Watch Commander, Sergeant Post, looked up from his desk and motioned them toward him.

"Where have you been?" he asked in a voice calculated to shout over a full gale. "I had everybody check. Too much trouble to keep in contact by radio, was it? Or was it even switched on? Don't tell me, I don't want to know. I even called your home, but your wife said you were still out."

"Did you wake her?"

Post looked apologetic.

"I had no choice," he said.

"Something important?"

The Watch Commander turned red with exasperation.

"Something important, he asks!" The volume of his voice was now enough to drown out the sound of a tornado. At least that is the way it seemed to those who were near. "Something important? Of course there is something important. Or do you think I have nothing better to do than try to track you down?" He did not wait for an answer, but added: "You're the ones who asked for news about Peter Shot, aren't you?"

"Yes," said Vledder, taking advantage of the fact that Post had to take a deep breath.

"Well, we found him," said the Watch Commander with a certain amount of satisfaction in his voice. He was so satisfied with himself, he even lowered the volume somewhat.

"Where?" asked DeKok.

"In an abandoned building near the Singel. Some junkie gave us a tip that he could be found there."

"Well, man, out with it. Did you arrest him? Is he in the cells? What did you do?"

Post shook his head.

"Nothing."

"Nothing?"

"Well, we called the Coroner, of course."

"Why?" asked Vledder.

"Because he was dead," said Meindert Post. Vledder was not the only one to have a tendency for stating the obvious.

15

For just a moment DeKok stared at Post as if he had not understood him. Then his eyebrows twitched slightly, but enough to make the Watch-Commander blink. Vledder saw from the expression on Meindert Post's face that DeKok had done something with his eyebrows, but when he looked at his partner he was too late to observe the phenomenon himself. He did observe that the news of Shot's death had upset his colleague somehow. Vledder thought he knew why. Peter Shot's death did not fit into any of the theories they had so far developed.

"Dead," said DeKok evenly.

Post nodded.

"I didn't see it myself, of course. But the report came over the radio. Apparently the patrol that discovered him, is thinking in terms of an overdose."

DeKok bit his lower lip.

"Have they moved the corpse yet?"

The Watch Commander shook his head.

"No, I gave instructions not to do anything until you arrived." He looked at the clock against the wall. "That's about an hour and a half ago. They're still with the corpse, in the dark," there was a slight overtone of censure in his voice. "That's way too long."

DeKok gave him a strange look.

"Too long?"

Post nodded vehemently.

"They're all just young people in my group, at the moment. Barely out of their teens. If it takes too long, they'll have nightmares because of this situation."

DeKok shrugged his shoulders.

"We've all had to get used to it."

The Watch Commander, despite his formidable exterior and his foghorn voice, betrayed a surprising amount of empathy.

"You . . . you," he roared, pointing an accusing finger at the gray sleuth, "you march across legions of corpses and won't lose a second's worth of sleep."

DeKok did not react in any visible way.

"What's the address?"

"Singel 812."

DeKok took Vledder by an elbow and turned away.

"Tell the children I'm coming," he tossed over his shoulder.

* * *

Back in the car, Vledder drove across the Dam and behind the Royal Palace. Without conscious thought he took every available shortcut and at speed.

"Why so fast?" asked DeKok suddenly.

Vledder laughed.

"You've the skin of an elephant."

DeKok shook his head.

"Strange . . . I always thought I was the most sensitive cop on the force."

"What do you mean?"

"Meindert . . . Meindert Post. Did you notice how upset he was?"

148

"Yes, because he could not reach us."

"That too, but that was only part of it. He cares about people and especially about those on his shift."

Vledder did not respond. At that moment they rounded the corner and arrived at the Singel. With screeching brakes they stopped in front of number 812. DeKok got out and looked up at the house. It was an old, somewhat dilapidated building that had been used as a warehouse for decades, from the time that the Singel Canal was still a center for transshipments from the larger coastal vessels to the barges that moved up the Rhine, even to Switzerland.

A marked police car, without lights, was parked in front of the door. Two young cops approached the aging Inspector. They really were young, thought DeKok, the male's cap visor was still shiny and the female did not look older than fifteen.

"We decided to wait in the car," said the young woman. It sounded like an apology.

DeKok nodded his understanding.

"Has a doctor been called?"

The male cop shook his head.

"No, sir, the Watch Commander told us not to do anything, just stand guard." He pointed upstairs. "There's nothing to be done, anyway. He must have been dead for a few days."

DeKok turned to Vledder.

"Alert the Herd."

The two young uniformed constables exchanged a meaningful glance. Even they had heard that DeKok routinely referred to the group of fingerprint experts, photographers and other specialists that invariable gathered on the scene of a violent death, as the *Thundering Herd*. Neither was old enough to know that the term referred to Woody Herman's band.

DeKok pointed vaguely in the direction of the two constables.

149

"One of you show me the exact location."

"Follow me, sir," said the young woman.

She pushed open the door and after a long, dank corridor, they reached a narrow, steep staircase. The old, loose treads creaked under their feet. In some places the treacherous railing had disappeared altogether. DeKok followed the young constable carefully. He was not at all sure that the stairs would support his more than 200 pounds.

On the third floor they entered a high, large room that seemed to stretch from the front of the house to the back. It was less dark here because some light penetrated through the tall, grimy windows. They cast long shadows on the walls which mixed with the moisture stains and other, more dubious spots on the walls. In some places the brick showed through the plaster and only a few shreds of wallpaper were here and there visible near the ceiling. The wooden floor had gaps which showed the joists, topped by menacing remnants of rusty nails, poised to trip the careless.

Faded hippie slogans were painted on the walls. "Flower Power," "Peace," and the inevitable "Today is the first day of the rest of your life." DeKok smiled a nostalgic smile. He had found that particular slogan so often in the past. In abandoned buildings, on fences, in youth hostels, in railroad stations and other likely and unlikely places, when the flower children still made Amsterdam one of their unofficial pilgrimage destinations. Where had they gone, he mused, the carefree generation that started every new day with new hope and a fresh cheerfulness. It may have been frustrating to a lot of people, but they brought a bright spot into the world, thought DeKok. Today nobody seemed to believe in love anymore, nobody believed in flowers anymore. His face fell. Only one flower had survived their idealistic ranting ... the poppy. The lovely poppy which hid such a world of endless misery behind its beauty. Another example of mankind's infinite ability to pervert loveliness and grace into ugly reality. The poppy was now the unseen decoration on the graves of hundreds of thousands of young people who should not have died before their time.

"Mr. DeKok," said the young woman, touching his arm. "Are you all right?"

The clear female voice broke his momentary reverie. She moved to the other end of the room, near one of the windows. The light of her flashlight illuminated a body on the floor. A handkerchief was delicately held in front of her nose. Then DeKok also noticed the smell.

He gave the young cop an encouraging smile and went to stand next to her, near the feet of the corpse. He looked down. The body was supine, at right angles to the wall. It looked like a relatively young man, thirty, maybe thirty-five years with thin flaxen hair and a sharply pointed nose above a slightly agape mouth. It was not a pleasant sight. Death had left its mark.

The cone of the flashlight moved and discovered a hypodermic to the right of the corpse as if slipped from a powerless hand.

DeKok stepped over the legs of the corpse and knelt down to the left of the dead man. Carefully he moved the sleeve of the jacket up . With his own flashlight he looked at the postmortem lividity on the arm and especially at the puncture marks in the hollow of the elbow. Some had been infected.

Slowly, painfully, DeKok came to his feet.

"Who identified him as Peter Shot?"

The young woman seemed slightly taken aback.

"Some junkie," shc said, hesitantly. "He reported it to the Watch Commander. He told him that he had found Peter Shot here, dead in this warehouse."

"Did he know we were looking for him?"

"Yes, he had heard that.

"Do you know who told him?"

The young woman shrugged.

"Apparently the junkie had heard it from a woman. Peter Shot owed her money. This woman asked a number of junkies to look out for Shot and to report him to the police at Warmoes Street."

"Do you know that junkie?"

"No, sir, I don't. But they will have his name at the station, I'm sure."

DeKok smiled.

"I'm sure, my dear," he said gently. "Tell me, how long have you been on the force?"

"I graduated four months ago."

"And your partner?"

"We were in the same class, sir."

DeKok looked surprised.

"And they sent you out together?"

"Not enough experienced constables to go around, I guess," answered the constable.

DeKok nodded.

"Well, you did very well, both of you," he said.

"Thank you, sir," blushed the woman. She started to put her handkerchief away.

"Don't bother," said DeKok, gesturing at her movement. "By all means keep your nose covered. You'll get used to it, eventually, but I know it isn't something pleasant."

The constable nodded, as if filing away the information, but her handkerchief disappeared in a breast pocket. There was a more determined look on her face.

They heard a noise from outside the room and a moment later the other constable entered, followed by Vledder and Dr. Koning, the Coroner.

Neither young constable showed by any expression that they were surprised at the appearance of the old doctor. In his striped pants, long swallow-tailed coat and a large, flamboyant Garibaldi hat, the Coroner looked as if he had just stepped out of the previous century.

DeKok approached the doctor and shook his hand heartily.

"You got here quick," he said.

Dr. Koning took off his hat and wiped his forehead with a large, red farmers handkerchief.

"We're busy tonight," he said tiredly. "I think it's the weather. Warm, depressing . . . as if waiting for a thunderstorm. I think this is the kind of weather when people don't really mind dying. I was in the neighborhood, a few blocks away . . . old couple . . . in their seventies . . . close together, leaning against a wall. Bible between them . . ."

"Suicide?"

The old Coroner nodded slowly.

"The old lady had cancer. Apparently hopeless. They must have saved all the painkillers they got on prescription. They must have been planning it for some time . . . those two. And tonight, both of them, went quietly sleeping into that dark night that comes for all of us. The son found them. The old man had repeatedly said that he couldn't face life without 'Mother.' Well they made sure." He remained silent, then added, "You see, our much touted *euthanasia on request* is not for everybody."

DeKok made a neutral sound.

"So," said the Coroner, a bit more brisk then before. "What have you got for me?"

DeKok pointed at the corpse.

"Another victim of heroin, I think."

Dr. Koning kneeled next to the dead man, keeping his hat in front of his chest. Then he reached out a hand and received DeKok's flashlight. Placing his hat on the floor, he lifted the eyelids and looked into the sightless eyes. He reached out again and DeKok retrieved his flashlight. Koning placed his hat back on his head and reached out another arm. Hastily Vledder came near and assisted the old man to his feet.

"Thank you, young man," said the Coroner. He turned toward DeKok.

"I would insist on a full autopsy," he counseled. "I think it may have been poisoned dope. I have seen several cases like this in the last few weeks. Apparently there is a large quantity of really bad dope . . . as if there's any good dope . . . anyway, there's lot of this very bad stuff around. Narcotics has been on it for a while . . . Inspectors Loet and Wolders."

"How long has he been dead?" asked DeKok.

Dr. Koning opened his mouth as if to protest. He did not like to give specific information at the scene of a crime. Then he shrugged, sighed and said: "At least thirty-six, maybe forty-eight hours. But, you know," he added, "that's just a rough estimate."

DeKok nodded soothingly.

"I'm much obliged, doctor. Do you think it could have been an overdose?"

"Almost certainly," answered the Coroner. "I think you'll find that will be the conclusion of the toxicological investigation. But it probably was just an added complication on top of the poisoned dope he had ingested earlier. Either way . . . he was beyond hope when he died."

For a while DeKok stared at the corpse, everybody else forgotten. Strange, he thought, at first I was shocked to hear of the death. Now it hardly seems to touch me. He tried to force his mind into the professional patterns that were required at a time like this, but was unable to do so. He tried to analyze his feelings, but gave it up with a sigh.

"He's officially dead?" he asked, almost brusque.

Vledder looked up in surprise. He had seldom heard that tone of voice and almost never in the presence of a corpse.

The Coroner, too, gave him a hard look.

"Yes, DeKok, he's officially dead," he said softly. Under Dutch Law a person was not really dead unless officially pronounced dead by a qualified member of the medical profession.

The Coroner turned around, preparatory to leaving, but the old Inspector tapped him on the shoulder.

"Just one moment, doctor," he said. He pointed at the young constables. "Please escort the doctor down. I want to make sure he reaches his pension."

Dr. Koning protested.

"I'm not as old as all that," he grumbled. But he stopped grumbling when the female constable took him by the arm and her partner deferentially lit the way with his flashlight.

The doctor had hardly left when there was loud stumbling on the stairs and soon thereafter Bram Weelen, one of the police photographers, was the first of the "Thundering Herd" to arrive. Instead of a flashlight he carried what looked like a portable searchlight. The strong, wide beam played over the grim surroundings.

"Hi, DeKok," greeted Weelen. "I must say, you pick the jolliest places to deposit corpses."

DeKok looked sorrowful.

"I don't deposit them," he said gravely. "Others do that for me."

Bram Weelen aimed his searchlight at the corpse.

"Is that the Peter Shot you've been looking for?"

"Apparently," said DeKok. "For the moment we'll have to accept that, but his identity is by no means confirmed."

"No papers?" asked Weelen.

"We haven't looked yet," said Vledder. "There seemed no hurry," he added, almost apologetically.

Bram Weelen mounted his searchlight by the simple expedient of extracting some telescoping legs. He then pushed a button somewhere and the source of the light was surrounded by a reflecting disk.

"Nifty, eh?" he asked proudly, while opening his aluminum suitcase. He took out his beloved Hasselblad camera and started to fit some lenses.

"The usual shots?" he asked, looking through the viewfinder.

DeKok smiled.

"The usual shots," he confirmed. "And," he added, "get me some special detail shot of the right side, with the hypodermic. Try to make the face shot presentable, if you can. I may need it for identification."

Weelen nodded to himself, took another, floor mounted light source from his suitcase and checked the flash attachment on his camera.

"Okidoki, here we go."

In rapid succession he made the required shots, apparently certain of the results. In a surprisingly short time he started to pack his gear again.

"I'm sure you'll want them tonight?" he asked, looking up at DeKok as he closed his suitcase.

"If it doesn't interfere with your marriage," agreed DeKok.

"Don't worry, nothing can interfere with that," said Weelen. He collapsed the legs on his searchlight and retracted the reflecting disk. With the suitcase in one hand and with what was now again an enormous flashlight in the other, he made his departure.

Ben Kruger, the fingerprint expert, entered as if on cue. He was followed by a number of other officers from the technical force. They immediately started to measure distances, angles and other pertinent data. Two of them started to string some yellow and red tape to isolate that part of the floor where the corpse was. More lights appeared and some officers started to look in the holes made by the missing planking. It seemed like a mob scene. But a mob with a purpose.

"Anything special?" asked Kruger, approaching DeKok after a long look around.

DeKok suddenly was irritated.

"That's for you to find out," he answered curtly. "You're the dactyloscopist."

Kruger gestured at the large room.

"Well, excuse me," he said. "I only asked because there must be thousands of prints in this area. You expect the killer's to be among them?"

DeKok did not answer. He approached the two young constables who had originally found the corpse.

"You two may go," he said.

The female shook her head.

"If it's all the same to you, sir, we would like to stay a little longer. We've never seen this type of operation."

For a moment DeKok hesitated. Then he looked at the eager expressions on the fresh young faces.

"All right," he said, "I'll square it with your boss."

Ben Kruger came up to DeKok. He tapped DeKok on the shoulder with his left hand. In his right hand he held a clamp wherein the hypodermic was securely fastened.

DeKok turned.

"Careful," warned Kruger, "moving the hypodermic away. If you were to hurt yourself with it, who knows the consequences." He raised the hypodermic in the air. "No good," he added.

"What's no good?"

157

"This thing, this needle."

"Out with it."

"No prints."

"Nothing?"

"No," said Kruger, "not even a smudge of one."

DeKok gave Vledder a meaningful glance and then turned around. Without another word he left. Vledder would follow up and make sure that those things that needed to be done, would be done. DeKok needed a long walk home. A long walk so he could think.

16

Vledder entered the detective room with a large plastic bag over one shoulder. He pushed an empty table against a wall and emptied the contents of the plastic bag on it. Among the clothes a weapon clattered onto the table. DeKok picked it up and weighed it in his hand. It was a small caliber revolver with an intricately carved handle and a short barrel.

"This was found on Peter Shot?"

Vledder nodded.

"In an ankle holster."

"I never noticed."

Vledder gestured at the weapon.

"We didn't find it until they took his clothes off at the lab. In one of his trousers pockets there was a handful of cartridges."

DeKok replaced the revolver on the table.

"Did you make arrangements to have it tested?"

"Yes. They'll be picking it up from here. I figured you wanted to compare the bullets fired from this, with the bullets found in the bodies of Martin Muller and Richard Sloten."

"Exactly."

"Well, if they match, we've solved the case."

DeKok ignored the remark.

"Did Kruger get any prints from the body?"

Again Vledder nodded.

"Yes. He promised to make a copy for transmittal to Detective Hollander in Houston. I already called Houston and told him the prints were on the way. They seemed happy about it and told us they would confirm as soon as possible."

DeKok stared at the table. The sparse, almost simple clothing intrigued him. The typical clothing of a junkie who spent little on anything else but his habit. What about the millions that had been stolen? Did they not make a difference. Would he not have spent some of it on a better set of clothes, a better place to live? Did he prefer to live like a homeless person, rather than use some of the wealth for creature comforts? But, in that case, why the robbery . . . that killing instinct? He sighed and looked at Vledder.

"Did you ask Kruger to compare Shot's prints with those found in Triangle Street?"

"Mrs. Sloten's house?"

DeKok nodded.

"Yes, I asked Kruger at the time to look for every possible print and to keep them in a separate file for the time being. Perhaps Shot's prints are among them. After all, while they were supposedly planning the robbery, they must have discussed it somewhere. Why not in Richard's house?"

"Supposedly planning?" asked Vledder.

"Mm," said DeKok. He went to his own desk and picked up an envelope. "Here are some shots of Peter's corpse. Bram Weelen just delivered them. I want you to check with Carmen Manouskicheck and see if she identifies him. Careful now," he admonished, "so she won't have to flush any of her merchandise away. After all," he smiled, "we actually have to thank her for finding Peter Shot so promptly. She must have mobilized all her junkies."

He remained silent for a while, staring out over the rooftops. Then a malicious twinkling appeared in his eyes as he turned around again.

"And show the pictures to Monika Buwalda." He grinned to himself. "Perhaps it will help her to see the dead killer of her fiancee." He pulled out his lower lip and let it plop back. "I'll take some copies to Lowee, myself."

Vledder gave him a searching look.

"You really think that's necessary?"

"Why?"

Vledder waved his hands.

"Well," he said, "I was thinking of the Penal Code . . . General Rules . . . Article ninety six . . ."

DeKok looked impatient.

"What's that Article . . . I left school some time ago."

Vledder raised a finger in the air, in an unconscious imitation of one of DeKok's many habits.

"The right to prosecute," he said didactically, "Is nullified by the death of the suspect."

"Aha," said DeKok. "I see where you're going. Now that Peter Shot is dead, we no longer have a case?"

"More or less. Of course we'll have to tie up the loose ends, but that's it."

DeKok looked at his young colleague. There was understanding and humor in his smile when he said: "We're just starting."

"What!?"

DeKok nodded slowly, thoughtfully.

"We've just added a problem, that's all."

Vledder looked nonplussed.

"What do you mean?"

DeKok took a photo from the envelope.

"Who killed Peter Shot?"

* * *

Commissaris Buitendam, DeKok's aristocratic chief, motioned with an elegant hand.

"Come in, DeKok," he said in his cultured voice. "I will not ask you to be seated, because I fear that the chances of your refusal are disproportionate."

He looked at his subordinate and tried a tentative, winning smile.

"But I would like to convey to you my satisfaction upon learning the news that this . . . eh . . . this Peter Shot has departed this vale of tears. That brings the case to a satisfactory conclusion, I think and has, in fact, justified the position taken by myself and the Judge-Advocate."

DeKok cocked his head, an unbelieving look in his eyes. For a long moment he stared at the Commissaris as if he was studying a strange insect.

"What exactly do you mean?" he asked finally.

The Commissaris seemed ill at ease.

"Well," he started, "well, it means of course, that the result of the investigations completely clears Messrs Houten and Busil. It proves that they have not the slightest connection to the robbery."

DeKok laughed in his most sarcastic way.

"I think that's a bit premature. One suspect, Peter Shot, is dead and he won't talk anymore. He can't tell us anymore where, and from whom, he received the information and to whom he was to make a possible payment of at least part of the loot in exchange." The gray sleuth made a dismissing gesture. "And what about the three million? Where did it go? So far, not a cent has been recovered."

He paused and took a deep breath.

"But . . ." said the Commissaris.

"Perhaps you don't like it," interrupted DeKok, "but as long as I don't know exactly how the robbery was planned, who was supposed to be involved in the sharing of the loot . . . for at least that long I reserve the right to continue my investigations in this case. And that includes, if necessary, an investigation into how one, or both, of the gentlemen you mentioned, are involved. Neither Houten, nor Busil, is above suspicion."

Outwardly the Commissaris remained calm.

"Last night," he began, "there was a burglary in the offices of Houten & Busil. Nothing is missing. The unwanted visitor, or visitors, has, or have, concentrated on searching some papers." He looked at DeKok. "Can you explain that?"

DeKok pursed his lips.

"Perhaps there are people who suspect that the three million is hidden there."

Commissaris Buitendam looked at DeKok for a long time. His face was serious, but did not betray any other emotion.

"This morning," he said finally, slowly, "I received an anonymous tip. The tipster seemed to indicate that you knew more about this burglary . . . even worse, he maintained that *you* had committed the burglary." He paused. Then he changed his tone of voice. "This is not the first time, DeKok, that I have had serious suspicions about your methods of investigation. I suspect that there are times that you exceed the limits of your authority."

DeKok stared at his boss with an innocent look.

"Well, that's my responsibility," he answered calmly. "If you can prove that I have exceeded my authority, I suggest you do so. Perhaps you'll get another *anonymous*," there was contempt in his voice as he emphasized the word, "tip to help you," he concluded.

Buitendam suddenly lost his temper. He slapped the top of his desk with a flat hand and rose from behind his desk.

"You're forbidden to continue with this case. You are *off* the case. Do you understand me?"

With difficulty DeKok kept his anger in check.

"Peter Shot's death is *not* the end of this case," he said, louder than he intended. "On the contrary, this is just the beginning. The man was killed in a very insidious way . . . he was literally doped to death. You cannot prohibit me from investigating the murder of Peter Shot." He took a deep breath, became calmer. "On what grounds?" he asked, "Incompetence?"

The Commissaris became angrier. There was a determined look on his face and his nostrils flared. His normally pale face became even paler.

"Your, your . . . your stubbornness drives me to despair," he finally managed to say.

DeKok nodded reasonably.

"Sure, sure," he said soothingly. "But," he continued, a hard tone in his voice, "you know what drives me to despair? The stupidity of people who are supposed to *lead* the police in their investigations."

Buitendam snorted.

"Whatever do you mean?"

"Stupidity," answered DeKok evenly. "Are you not familiar with the word?"

The Commissaris, as so often in the past, lost the last amount of reserve.

"OUT!!" he roared.

DeKok left.

* * *

Vledder shook his head, a mock disapproving look on his face.

"Really . . . to accuse the Commissaris of stupidity. It's reckless, that's what it is. Why do you always wind up quarreling with him. One of these days he'll win the argument and you'll be out of a job. Anyway . . . this time he's right. Peter Shot's death closes the case."

DeKok looked indulgent.

"And how do you figure that?"

"Simple, as I said before. Peter Shot was the last suspect to be alive. All the others are also dead. Richard Sloten and Peter committed the robbery. In order to get rid of incriminating witnesses and, incidentally, keep all the loot himself, Peter first shot Martin Muller. Then he killed Richard and finally Richard's mother who, we can assume, was fully informed of the plans."

"Fine. And who killed Peter Shot?"

Vledder smiled.

"But that is a different case altogether. I'm sure the underworld was fully aware that Peter Shot was in possession of a large amount of money, some three million as you'll recall. Well, as soon as that became more or less general knowledge . . . it was open season on Peter Shot."

DeKok sank down in the chair behind his desk. He rubbed the tip of his nose and then raised a finger in the air. For a few moments he stared at the finger as if he had never seen it before. Then he pointed it at Vledder.

"So, according to you, some wise guys first located Peter Shot, killed him with an overdose and then took off with the loot?"

"Something like that, yes."

DeKok grinned triumphantly.

"And how," he asked sweetly, "did Peter Shot carry all that money around. In a large plastic bag? In a knapsack?"

Vledder shook his head.

"That's a deliberate simplification," he said patiently. "I'm sure that Peter had hidden the money very carefully. But . . . and this is important . . . he was the only one who knew. Therefore, as long as he held the secret, his death was of no use to anybody. On the contrary ... only a living Peter Shot could reveal the whereabouts of the money."

DeKok looked thoughtful.

"You mean that his death automatically also means that somebody else now has the money, or knows where it is."

Vledder nodded vehemently.

"But of course! And that's why I think the Commissaris is right ... this once. The robbery case is finished. Closed. We have a *new* case ... who killed Peter Shot? And who has the money?"

DeKok did not answer. Slowly he rose from his chair and started to pace in the limited space available. His hands were on his back, his head was bowed and his eyes seemed closed. Without conscious effort he avoided any obstacles and his mind ignored the noises around him. He was dissatisfied with the entire case. He had a strange, restless feeling that all theories were somehow lacking ... that they were contrary to the facts. In direct opposition to the stark truth ... *he knew*! Somewhere in the recesses of his mind, hidden behind veils of superfluous events was hidden the answer he sought. The solution was in his head, if he could only identify it.

He stopped in front of the window. Diagonally across was Corner Alley and he could just see the slight bend in the ancient little street that led to *Our Dear Lord in the Attic*, a hidden church now restored as a museum.

The alley always stank of rotted fish, mingled with the stench of stale beer and liquor. The stink would permeate the police station and surrounding buildings. In the police station the aromas were additionally mingled with the sickening, sweetish smell of the disinfectants, used to regularly clean the cells in the basement.

How many times had he stood here, balancing on the balls of his feet while thinking over the implications of a particular

166

case. Every time again, and again, when he thought he had seen it all, crime reared its ugly head in a new guise, a different manifestation. Every time, sooner or later, he had been able to come up with a solution. But he was getting older and his poor brain was tired. He pressed his eyes closed and tried to shake away the mists that seemed to cloud his thinking. He was not successful. With a sigh he turned toward Vledder.

"You know," he said slowly, "I am not at all convinced that Peter Shot had anything to do with the robbery in the first place."

Vledder was astonished.

"You don't mean it."

DeKok shrugged.

"I just can't put the pieces together," he admitted.

Vledder came nearer and placed a hand on the old man's shoulder.

"You're getting old, DeKok," he said gently. He raised a folder he had been holding. "This is the ballistics report."

"Well?"

Vledder grinned.

"Martin Muller, Richard Sloten and his mother were all killed with bullets from Peter Shot's revolver."

17

They passed the barrier downstairs, gave a jovial wave to the Sergeant on duty and passed out of the police station into Warmoes Street. DeKok walked up front, his threadbare jacket with the leather patches on the elbows topped by the decrepit little hat, jauntily pulled down over one ear. An envelope with pictures was clamped under one arm. Vledder followed, a little more formal, neat and trim in a stylish suit with matching necktie. His blond hair parted to perfection.

They strolled through the Quarter until they reached Rear Fort Canal. It was busy. Men waited in lines in front of the sex theaters and not a single whore was unoccupied. It was warm, brooding weather and it seemed to increase the mood of heightened sexuality.

DeKok stopped suddenly. He had discovered a herring cart. He approached, a gleam in his eyes. He watched with undisguised greed as the herring man deftly scaled a raw herring, divested it of head and intestines, removed the spine and placed the filets, still attached by the tail on a plate. DeKok grabbed it by the tail almost before the man had released the fish. Briefly the old sleuth dragged the herring through the chopped, raw onions and then, with head bent far back, he let the fish slide down. Two, maybe three bites and only the tail was left. He disposed of the tail in the proper receptacle and took another herring. He had finished two of the delicacies before Vledder had taken a bite from his first fish. By the time Vledder disposed of his first tail, DeKok had finished his third herring. With a look of regret he eyed the tempting platter of raw fish, then shook his head and unearthed the necessary coins to pay for his treat. Both Vledder and DeKok were totally unaware that tourists would gape and shiver in wonder as the Dutch casually consumed tons of the raw fish each year.

They rinsed their hands in a basin containing water and vinegar and dried them on a conveniently provided cloth. Then they walked on.

Still with a satisfied look on his face, DeKok turned to his younger partner.

"Has Monika Buwalda seen Peter's pictures yet?"

Vledder shook his head.

"Mark Stoops is going by there this evening. He has a set of prints."

DeKok nodded to himself.

"And Carmen Manouskicheck?"

"I haven't been there yet."

They crossed the bridge near Stove Alley and entered Little Lowee's bar. Inside it was cool, dark and intimate.

Little Lowee greeted them with a happy smile.

"Been awhile," he exclaimed.

DeKok hoisted himself onto a barstool at the end of the bar and leaned against the wall. This gave him a complete overview of the bar. Young Vledder took the stool next to his old colleague. It was relatively quiet inside. Most of the tables were vacant and they were the only ones at the bar.

Lowee wiped his hands on a cloth.

"Same recipe?" he asked.

Patiently DeKok watched as Little Lowee performed his traditional ritual. Only after he had savored the first sip of the excellent cognac, did he pull the photos from the envelope and showed them to the diminutive barkeeper.

Little Lowee studied them with care. Then he looked up. His face was pale.

"Tha's . . . tha's Peter Shot," he said.

DeKok nodded gloomily.

"Peter Shot," he repeated, "found in an abandoned building on the Singel."

Lowee shook his head.

"He don't look good."

Vledder grinned.

"He's dead."

Lowee ignored Vledder. As usual, he tolerated DeKok's partner, but that did not mean he would engage in conversation with him.

"He look dead," said Lowee, as if Vledder had not spoken. "But he done lost some weight," he continued. "I usta knows him when he were much thicker . . . fatter face, you see."

"When did you see him last?" asked DeKok.

"I tole ye that before, I did . . . coupla months ago . . . mebbe two months ago."

DeKok took another swallow of cognac.

"You told me then that he pulled a gun, here in the bar."

"Exactum, I tole you . . . coupla months."

"What did it look like?"

"What?"

"The gun."

Lowee shrugged.

"Revolver . . . notta pistol . . . short barrel . . . real pimp model."

"Would you recognize the weapon?"

"Mebbe, mebbe not . . . you got it?"

"No, it's still in the lab."

Lowee again studied Peter Shot's photographs.

"How diddee croak?"

"Overdose, we think"

"Get outta here . . . overdose?"

DeKok nodded.

"Administered by a party, or parties unknown. Probably while he was already passed out from a previous shot."

"You knows anybody?"

DeKok laughed.

"No, we're trying to figure that out." He leaned closer over the bar. "We would also like to know what happened to the three million," he whispered. He looked at Lowee and then added: "Perhaps . . . you . . . What do you think?"

Lowee grinned back.

"Notta word about the loot. I doesn't think you gotta look around here . . . amongst the regulars, so to speak. Peter Shot and his caper weren't no never mind of none of us." He realized what he had just said. Of course, DeKok knew that he fenced on the side, but that was no reason to brag about it. Confused, he replaced the photos on the bar. "You knows," he began hastily, "I done some thinking about this here robbery, you knows and I thinks you're all wet."

"How's that?"

"I just cain't believe it nohow."

"Go on."

Lowee now had a disgusted look on his face. He tapped the photos with an index finger.

"I just cain't believe datta slick number like Richard, Slick Ricky that were, datta a slick guy like that was gonna set up a deal with a loser like Shot. I knows me customers and I just cain't believe it." he looked at DeKok, his friendly, mousy face cocked

over one shoulder. "I tells you, DeKok, as far as I's concer . . .
conc . . . Iffen you asks me, Slick Ricky never even knowed this
Peter Shot."

* * *

From Lowee's Bar they walked through Barn Alley to New
Market and then via Emperors Street to Crooked Ditch Canal.
Near a hidden foot bridge behind King Street, DeKok waited and
looked up at the facade of the house.

"I hope she's coherent."

"What do you mean?" asked Vledder.

"Poor old Carmen has been addicted so long. She
sometimes is so stoned that a sensible word is simply out of the
question."

They crossed the street. In front of the door with the peeling
paint he looked up again. Only after he had seen the shadow of a
woman flicker in the little spy mirror outside the window, did he
push open the door. Again they climbed the rickety stairs,
Vledder following resignedly.

She waited for them at the top of the stairs, a welcoming
smile on her ruined face.

"So, you're back again," she greeted.

DeKok smiled back.

"I want to show you something." He passed by her and
entered the room. He spread out the photos on the table.

Curious, Carmen Manouskicheck came closer and leaned
over the photos. After a while she straightened up and looked at
the Inspector.

"Why are you doing this to me?" she asked. "Do you want
me to know what I'll look like in a year or so?"

DeKok shook his head.

"Not at all. I just want to know if you can identify him."

"Sure," she said slowly, "that's Peter Shot."

"Do you notice anything about him?"

Again Carmen studied the photographs. Then she shrugged her shoulders.

"One more dead junkie . . . what else is there to say?"

"Don't you think he's skinny?"

She grinned without mirth.

"Ever seen a fat junkie?"

DeKok placed a gentle hand on her shoulder.

"Carmen," he said patiently, "when Peter was here last he . . ."

". . . he looked better than now," she completed the sentence.

DeKok smiled approvingly.

"How did he use his dope? Do you know?"

"He shot up."

"Just the needle?"

She made a vague gesture.

"Well, he was the type of guy that would try anything. I'm sure he also sniffed and smoked."

"But you don't know for sure?"

"No. Not for sure."

DeKok replaced the photographs in the envelope, took Vledder by an arm and started to leave. Near the door he turned around.

"Carmen . . . take care of yourself." There was concern in his voice.

Carmen leaned against the table. With a tired gesture she wiped the lusterless hair away from her face.

"When will I see you again? Next time you find a corpse?"

"No."

"Will you come to my funeral?"

DeKok looked at her for several seconds. Then he nodded slowly.

"I will come to your funeral."

A tired smile played around her lips.

"Then there will be at least one," she said softly.

* * *

They more or less retraced their steps to Warmoes Street. DeKok did not talk. His mood was somber. In his mind he heard the words spoken by Little Lowee. The little barkeeper was right. For some time, he too, had had the feeling that he was on the wrong track with this particular investigation. He asked himself how it could have happened. As far as he knew, he had been his usual self, had followed every clue and taken everything into account. What frustrated him more than he could say, was the firm conviction that he had all the necessary facts to come to the correct conclusion, if only he could get back to the point where he had started to follow the wrong trail. He looked at Vledder.

"When is the autopsy?"

Vledder shook his head, apparently interrupted in his own musings.

"Tomorrow morning," he said after a slight hesitation. "That's the earliest they could schedule it."

DeKok rubbed his chin.

"Ask them to look particularly at the cerebellum."

Vledder looked confused.

"The cerebellum?"

DeKok nodded.

"Yes, perhaps it is spongy."

"Spongy?"

"Yes," said DeKok, slightly irritated. "Spongy, weakened, softened, disintegrated, whatever."

"All right, all right," said Vledder hastily, "but why?"

"Sorry," said DeKok, "I did not have a chance to tell you."

"Tell me what?" Vledder could be irritating at times.

"Because of what Dr. Koning said about the poisoned heroin, I called Inspector Loet of Narcotics. He told me that he and Wolders have been trying to trace the origin of the poisoned dope for some time. Apparently . . . and this is all they are sure of at the moment . . . a large quantity of street quality heroin has been diluted with this poison."

"So, that should be noticeable, I think."

"Not really. Apparently the poison in combination with the heroin becomes virtually undetectable to the user."

"What is it?"

"That they don't know either. They have been unable to isolate it in the labs."

Vledder was amazed.

"But how is that possible?"

"You might well ask. Everybody is asking the same question. All they know is that the results are catastrophic. The incubation period, so to speak, is being estimated at about three weeks. Then the first symptoms appear . . . headaches, slurred speech. Eyesight diminishes also. Eventually the entire motor control of the body just atrophies. The victims are unable to do anything at all. They can't read, can't write, can't grip anything. Control of the large limbs disappears first along with a complete loss of discernment. The inevitable result is death. At this very moment there are tens, maybe hundreds of victims in various stages of dying because of it. They are spread over several hospitals."

"You're right, that *is* catastrophic."

DeKok nodded.

"And can nothing be done?" asked Vledder.

"No," answered DeKok.

"And they die because of a spongy cerebellum?"

"No, they die because of a complete breakdown of all bodily functions. But in all the victims they have found a deteriorated cerebellum . . . spongy, if you like."

Vledder shuddered.

"The strange thing is," continued DeKok, "that apparently the symptoms do not appear when the heroin is administered directly into the blood stream. Only when sniffing, or smoking the foul stuff, does it take effect. It seems that it needs to be warmed to a certain temperature before entering the body. That, heat I mean, is the catalyst for the poison."

Vledder nodded to himself.

"That's why you asked Carmen how Peter Shot used his dope."

"Exactly. If the autopsy shows the expected deterioration of the cerebellum, then that will be the consequence of a process that has been going on for some time."

"How long?"

"Several weeks, at least."

Vledder stopped suddenly.

"But," he said, "if that's true it also means he couldn't possibly have had anything to do with the robbery."

"Exactly," answered DeKok. "Peter Shot would have been physically incapable of doing so."

18

With a portentous face Vledder picked up the sheet of paper on which he had been writing.

"Peter Vanderberg," he read in the tone of a school teacher, "also known as Peter Shot, was born in DenBos some thirty five years ago as the second son of a construction worker and a farmer's daughter from Brabant. While he was still an infant, his parents emigrated to Canada where his father found a job in Hamilton, Ontario."

DeKok looked over at Vledder.

"And where," he asked "did you gather this illuminating prose?"

Vledder looked insulted.

"It is," he said haughtily, "my condensation of what I have learned about Peter Shot."

"All right, go on."

Vledder cleared his throat.

"When Peter was barely nineteen, Canadian soil became too hot for him. He already had a number of convictions on his record and the police were looking for him in connection with a new crime. He moved to the United States and wound up in Chicago. During an ordinary bar fight he pulled a pistol and shot a couple of bullets into the stomach of the bar owner. The man survived, but Peter spent several years in jail. Before the end of his sentence, he escaped from prison and fled back to Chicago."

"What was he? In his mid twenties?"

"Yes, and for a long time he remained in hiding. At least, there are no reports of any additional criminal activities. But then he suddenly surfaced in Houston and was involved in a number of burglaries and some armed robberies. During one such incident he shot a cop who tried to arrest him. The policeman was fatally injured and died on the way to the hospital. His wanted poster was updated to included *Armed and Dangerous*. Although he was spotted a number of times, he managed to elude the American police."

"What is the source of all this information?"

"Detective-Inspector Hollander of Houston. He matched the fingerprints we sent and that led him to the *Vanderberg* file. I added some research from here in Holland. There are some relatives, uncles and aunts, still alive in and around DenBos and Brabant . . . law-abiding citizens without a blemish, all of them."

"And?"

"What do you mean?"

"What else is there?"

Vledder made an apologetic gesture.

"You know the rest. Peter Shot surfaces in Amsterdam, boasts about his criminal past and dies because of an overdose of heroin. I also received a report from Kruger. Kruger seems convinced that Peter could not have administered the last shot, the shot that killed him, himself."

"So?"

"Yes, because then his fingerprints would have been on the hypodermic, you see. And it was clearly wiped clean. Whoever gave Peter his last shot, must have wiped off the hypodermic and put it there."

"I had already figured that much myself."

"So it was murder, after all," said Vledder with his penchant for stating the obvious.

"Undoubtedly," said DeKok, irked. "What about the other prints?"

"What other prints?"

"Shot's fingerprints," explained DeKok patiently. "Did Kruger compare them with the prints found at the Sloten house?"

"Oh, that. Yes, it took some time, but you know how precise Kruger always is. Anyway, there was nothing . . . nothing that even looked like a match."

DeKok sat down on the edge of Vledder's desk.

"And the most important part?"

"You mean the cerebellum?"

"Yes."

Vledder swallowed.

"Spongy, destroyed."

For a long time they both remained silent. Outside the constant noise of the Red Light District penetrated into the detective room and at times overwhelmed the noises in the room itself. One of the overhead lights started to hum, as if a ballast was about to give out. Vledder took a long ruler from his desk and reached up. A sharp tap resulted in diminished noise, but two of the four tubes went out as well. He replaced the ruler and sat down again.

"Dr. Rusteloos pointed the brain out to me," said Vledder suddenly, It was easy to see, even to my untrained eyes. According to the good doctor, the first symptoms must have appeared weeks ago."

DeKok sighed.

"That removes every shred of doubt. There is no way he could have been involved in the robbery."

Vledder shook his head.

"No, no way. I was really impressed . . . no, that's not the word I'm looking for. It was a terrible sight. An autopsy is never any fun, but to see a brain so totally destroyed . . . it's . . . it's horrible."

"Yes," said DeKok. "And the most terrible part of it is that the poison only hastens the process. In the long run all dope does the same. It attacks the body, the brain and the end is always inevitable."

"But with all that we're just as far from a solution as we were before," said Vledder. "Perhaps further. At least I had the illusion that it was just a matter of finding Peter Shot and we would be done." He snorted. "Well, we *have* Peter Shot and there is no way he could have been involved. Where does that leave us?"

DeKok nodded.

"As I said before . . . with one more murder."

Vledder made a fist and banged the top of his desk.

"But how is that possible? How did we arrive at Peter Shot in the first place? And who could be so interested in his death that they helped him along when his imminent death was a foregone conclusion?"

DeKok smiled sadly.

"Death comes to us all," he said. "But the killer could not wait."

Vledder looked at him.

"Any idea of a motive."

"Sure," answered DeKok, "three million of them."

Vledder was puzzled.

"But," he protested, "Peter Shot could not have done the robbery . . . he had no connection to the loot."

DeKok smiled knowingly.

"Think about it," he said. Then he got up and went over to the coat rack. Vledder followed him.

"Where are you going?"

DeKok placed his little, ridiculous hat on his head.

"I'm going to see Karstens," he said. "I want to know if my painting is ready."

* * *

It was a wonderful, soft summer night and the old elms along the canals stood motionless, except for a soft rustling of the leaves as a stray puff of air, or a bird, passed by. High above the ancient rooftops, stars twinkled in a cloudless sky. DeKok hummed an old song about love and death while he searched his pockets for something sweet. He finally found a small bag with a few pieces of licorice left in it. He popped the three, or four, pieces in his mouth and deposited the empty bag in a trash can. Despite the setbacks, he did not feel discouraged and he wondered why. His good humor had reasserted itself and seemed to increase when he saw Vledder's depressed face.

"What's the matter," he asked with a mouth full of licorice.

Vledder shook his head as if to clear the cobwebs.

"I can't make any connections," he admitted. "That horrible brain keeps preying on my mind."

DeKok grimaced.

"All the more reason to make sure your own brain stays clean," he advised cheerfully. "You might need it some time, being a policeman, you see."

Vledder bit his lower lip in frustration.

"But *who* killed Peter Shot and *why?*" he exclaimed.

DeKok laughed.

"You've asked that before, I think."

"Yes," answered Vledder angrily. "And I will keep on asking it until I have an answer."

DeKok shrugged.

"I'm not all that disappointed," he said carelessly. "Peter Shot's death *does* open a number of new perspectives."

"Such as?"

"If we can find *his* killer, then we would also know who killed Martin Muller, Slick Ricky and his mother *and* who did the robbery."

Vledder shook his head, still angry.

"I can't see that."

"But it is so simple," said DeKok, swallowing the last of his licorice and continuing in a clearer voice: "It is a matter of combining what we know. You see, there's the revolver we found on Peter Shot. The same weapon, according to the lab, that was involved in the other three murders. We also know that Peter could not have used the weapon that way."

"His motor control was shot to hell," muttered Vledder.

"Yes, indeed, he was unable to function properly," corrected DeKok gently.

Vledder walked on, deep in thought. Then his face cleared.

"You're right," he exclaimed. "I'm beginning to see the connection. The killer of Peter Shot is the same as the guy from the robbery and the other killings. But ... he didn't just kill Peter, he also left the weapon with the corpse."

DeKok patted him on the shoulder.

"Perhaps it was even Peter's weapon that has been used by the killer. Maybe we can find that out from Lowee, he might recognize it. But no matter what ... the entire thing has been very shrewdly put together. If the real killer's plans had succeeded, then we would have buried Peter Shot, also known as Peter Vanderberg, with the full conviction that we had buried the man who did the robbery."

"And the real killer could have enjoyed his three million in peace and contentment, secure in the knowledge that all leads to him would have been obliterated."

"Exactly," said DeKok.

"Actually," said Vledder after a while, reflecting, "we have to thank old Kruger for the idea that it went the way it went."

"Yes," agreed DeKok. "And we should also thank Dr. Koning who put the idea of the poisoned dope in my head."

They walked on. Vledder kept shaking his head from time to time, but this time not to clear it of cobwebs, but more in wonder at the unusual set of circumstances and coincidences that had brought them to this point.

Suddenly he stopped.

"It must have been well planned." He gesticulated with his arms. "There's no other way. The real killer must have heard of Shot's reputation. He had been bragging everywhere what a ruthless criminal he was and what he had done in the States, even killed a cop. That reputation must have given the killer the idea to serve Peter up on a platter, so to speak." He clucked in admiration. "Very, very clever."

DeKok looked at his enthusiastic partner.

"Take it one step further," he instructed.

"Eh, what?"

DeKok laughed.

"You made such a good start . . . now take it one step further."

"I don't understand . . . what do you mean?"

DeKok closed one eye and rubbed the side of his nose.

"Who served up Peter on a platter, as you so colorfully expressed?"

For a moment Vledder seemed lost in thought. Then he looked up, understanding lighting up his face.

"Monika . . . Monika Buwalda."

185

19

Maria, Karstens's friend, lover and favorite model opened the door for the two detectives. She was dressed in a G-string and a broad smile. She held the door wide open with one hand and made no attempt to cover herself.

"Well, well," she said mockingly, "if I had known it was the cops, I would have worn something less formal."

Vledder blushed, which seemed to amuse the girl very much.

"Should you be dressed like this, or rather undressed, when you answer the door?" asked DeKok.

"But why not? I can wear what I want in my own house."

"Yes, but what if someone sees you when you open the door?"

"Oh well," she shrugged, her magnificent breasts jiggling slightly. Vledder seemed fascinated, but DeKok appeared not to notice. "That's the chance they take," she continued, "if they don't want to see me, they shouldn't ring my doorbell."

"May we come in?"

"But of course, Inspector." she stepped aside and allowed the cops to enter. She closed the door behind them and squeezed past them on her way into the house.

"Come along," she tossed over her shoulder, "he's in the back."

For a moment the two men admired her graceful figure as she walked, barefoot and unconcerned toward the back of the corridor. Then they followed.

Peter Karstens seemed happily surprised when the cops entered.

"DeKok," he exclaimed jovially, "I had expected you earlier. Come in and make yourself at home. We were just about to open a bottle of wine . . . it looks like a wonderful Burgundy from an excellent year." He laughed happily. "Or maybe an excellent wine from a wonderful year . . . who can tell?" He pointed at Vledder. "I see you brought your henchman."

DeKok shook his head, suppressing a smile.

"I don't care much for your choice of words," he said. "Dick Vledder is hardly a henchman."

Karstens grinned amiably.

"Well, what can I say. It's my nature. You know what I think about Law, Order, Government and all that hoopla. In the best of circumstances perhaps a necessary evil . . . with special emphasis on *evil*."

DeKok did not react. He felt little inclined to a fruitless discussion regarding the necessities of Law and Order and its associated requirements. Karstens and DeKok were of too varied an opinion about that. DeKok's Calvinistic upbringing almost forced him to be a certain way and Peter Karstens' outlook on life was too chaotic to be easily acceptable to the Inspector. And yet there was a definitive bond between the two, so diametrically opposed characters. A bond created by mutual respect.

He looked around and saw Maria disappear in the back. Her naked figure like a lovely nymph in the twilight of the forest as she drifted away between stacks of paintings and easels.

Karstens pointed at a long, rough-hewn table on which were some candles, a bottle and two glasses.

"Give me a second and I'll get some more glasses."

He busied himself at a sideboard and at that time Maria re-appeared, carrying a tray with cheeses. She had dressed herself. In the dim light of the candles her beauty took on an extra dimension of loveliness. Her figure was draped in a long, black skirt from which her bare feet peeked out as she walked. She had also put on a low-cut blouse that barely concealed her bosom. Her long hair fell in waves over the creamy shoulders. All three men stopped and stared as she came closer. DeKok heard Vledder hold his breath.

With a gracious gesture she offered the plate. Karstens took it from her and placed it on the table.

"You've met Maria?" said the painter.

"Yes," said DeKok, "we know her."

Vledder blushed again, but Maria looked at the old man with a twinkle in her eyes.

"Inspector," she said, "you only *think* you know me. You have merely *seen* me, which is not the same thing at all, believe me."

Her voice had changed. It sounded sensual, it exuded promise and yet seemed chaste at the same time. The total effect was enough to mesmerize any man.

Karstens looked on, obviously impressed as well.

"Maria," he said thoughtfully, "comes from a long line of witches. There's no other explanation. You better be careful, you'll be enslaved before you know it." He motioned toward DeKok and went to a covered canvas in the corner. He whipped away the cover and revealed the painting. "There you go . . . your painting."

For several minutes DeKok looked in admiration. He recognized Maria in a dance pose which openly, yet delicately emphasized her beauty and grace. The skirt, the blouse, the boots ... they all matched exactly the color and patterns of the costumed doll, exactly as it was recorded in his memory. But the lifeless doll had been transformed into a living, breathing vision of loveliness.

"Beautiful, Peter," said DeKok at last. "Really exquisite. If my government salary allowed it, I would buy it from you."

"For you," laughed the painter, "a special price." Before DeKok could raise a protest, Karstens added: "A crate of good wine."

Smiling, they shook hands on the deal.

"I know what you like," said DeKok.

They sat down around the table. Maria served the wine and handed the platter of cheese around. Although she was at the fringes, she seemed to be the center of the small gathering. When she finally sat down with the men, she became the undisguised focus of the others.

DeKok sipped his wine and nodded approvingly. For a while nobody said a word and enjoyed in silence. After Karstens had poured the second round, DeKok looked at Maria.

"There's a burning question my colleague wants to ask you," he said.

"Yes," said Maria simply.

DeKok shook his head.

"It's not what you think. I'll let him ask you himself." His eyes twinkled mischievously. "That is, if he has regained the power of speech."

Maria turned her dazzling gaze toward Vledder.

"Never mind the Inspector," she said, "he likes to tease." This time she sounded like an older sister. "Go ahead, ask me," she added.

"Well, yes," said Vledder. "I wanted to know if you ever worked for Houten & Busil, the trucking company."

190

Maria shook her head decisively.

"Never."

Peter Karstens seemed confused.

"But," he said, "you told me about the plan for the robbery."

"Yes, I told you that."

Peter looked at her with narrowed eyes.

"But didn't that plan come from the offices of Houten & Busil?"

"I'm sure it did."

Vledder swallowed.

"Then how did you come to know about it?" he asked.

The girl seemed surprised and disinterested.

"I heard about it . . . from another girl. I used to meet her every now and then at the office of the Temp Service for whom we both worked. When it so happened, we would go out for a cup of coffee, or something. She had found the plan in the office. It was in the drawer of a desk. She joked about it. 'If you could only find a man who dared,' she said."

DeKok gave her a winning smile.

"And that's when you thought of Peter here?"

"Oh," she said, "that was months later. It happened to come up in conversation when we were low on wine again."

"What was the name of that girl?" asked Vledder.

She looked at him.

"Monika."

"Was the last name Buwalda?"

She smiled.

"I never asked her last name."

* * *

Impatiently Vledder paced up and down in the space so often used by DeKok.

"We *have* to arrest her."

"Who?" asked DeKok calmly.

"Monika . . . Monika Buwalda."

"On what grounds?"

"On what grounds?" Vledder sounded exasperated. "On what grounds? Isn't it obvious that she's involved up to her neck?"

DeKok nodded slowly.

"More than likely. But what can we charge her with? Accessory . . . before, or after the fact? Not so easy to prove."

Vledder made a dismissing gesture.

"Right from the start she misled us. She made us believe that Peter Shot had committed the robbery."

DeKok grinned ruefully.

"So? Isn't that allowed? There isn't a single statute that prohibits that." He leaned back in his chair and looked at Vledder who had stopped in front of his desk. "As far as we know, what exactly is her role in all this? She came of her own free will to this office and told us that her fiancee, Richard Sloten, and Peter Shot had committed the robbery. She also told us that she had been present at some of the planning sessions. But other than that we don't have a thing to charge her with . . . not a single concrete action." He sighed and pushed his chair a little further back. Then he placed his feet on the desk.

"Go on," urged Vledder.

"Very well. After Maria's revelations last night I thought for a moment about the possibility of tempting someone into the job . . . inducing to commit a crime, you see. I rejected that, however."

"Why?"

"Well, if the robbery had been committed in the way it had been described in the plan, then . . ."

"You mean, the way Karstens wanted to do it, by exchanging armored trucks?"

DeKok nodded.

"The actual robbery was totally different, however . . . much more direct . . . much more violent. And that is the question, you see. Who provided that extra element?"

Vledder hesitated.

"Maybe it was Peter Shot after all. Perhaps the plan was his and then he was replaced at the last moment, when it was clear that he was physically not in any shape to participate."

DeKok shook his head.

"No, no. If Peter Shot had really been involved, Monika would never have mentioned his name."

Vledder was not convinced.

"Why not? She also named Richard Sloten and he *was* involved."

DeKok pressed his lips together, a disapproving look on his face. After a while he answered.

"Yes, she did," he said, "but only *after* she already knew that Richard was dead."

Vledder sat down behind his desk. Only then did he ask the next question.

"What? Are you sure?"

DeKok nodded, but before either of them could say anything else, Mark Stoops approached their desks.

"I showed those pictures to the gal in Dovecote," he announced.

"Monika Buwalda?"

"Yep, just like Vledder asked me."

"Well?"

"What a broad . . . what an attitude . . . such arrogance. If I earned in a year what she pretends in an hour, I'd retire tomorrow."

DeKok laughed.

"How did she react?"

"She seemed a bit nervous. But that means little, of course. My wife would also get nervous if I were to show her some pictures of a dead guy." He threw the envelope with photographs on DeKok's desk. "That's Peter Shot," he added.

"Is that what she said?"

"Yes."

"No more?"

Stoops grinned behind his luxurious moustache.

"Oh yes. *I'm glad that filthy beast finally killed himself,* she added."

"Did you tell her it was an overdose?"

Stoops shook his head.

"No. I just showed her the pictures and asked her if she knew the man."

"So, she did not ask how he died?"

"No . . . it's crazy . . . but I had the distinct impression she already knew that."

* * *

Vledder happily drove the old VW through the busy center of Amsterdam. He was glad to be behind the wheel again, even if it was the same old car. There had been much too much walking lately, he reflected. DeKok was seated in the passenger seat and held the painting in his lap. He again admired the subtle artistry of his radical friend as he contemplated the vivid colors . . . the white, open blouse with the delicate embroidery . . . an exuberant rose with colorful ribbons . . . the wide skirt with cornflowers along the hem . . . and Maria's sensuous body to bring it all to startling realism.

"Peter Karstens," he said with conviction, "is a great artist."

Vledder glanced aside.

"What do you expect to do with that painting?"

"No need to speak in such a doubtful voice, young Vledder," said DeKok. Vledder merely snorted. "You see," continued DeKok reasonably. "I have never been completely satisfied with the mystery of the disappearing doll. Why did the killer take that doll? I think it was a mistake."

"Why?" asked Vledder, keeping his full attention on the road and presenting a clumsy bicyclist with a short blast of the horn.

"The killer was too careful," answered DeKok, still studying the painting. He had not seen the bicyclist and had ignored the sound of the horn.

"I don't understand."

"I think," said DeKok, slouching further down into the narrow seat, "I think that the killer was afraid that the doll might have led to a trail in his direction. But if he had just left the doll where it was, I would never have paid any attention to it. After all, it's not all that special. Many houses have costumed dolls. It's a favorite tourist purchase."

Vledder found a parking place near the travel agency that specialized in trips to Germany and Eastern Europe. They entered and DeKok showed the painting to the woman behind the desk.

"Where do they wear this?"

"You mean the costume?"

"Yes."

She glanced in the direction of the office.

"I don't know," she said. "I'll ask my boss."

She got up and went to the office. After a few seconds she returned with a small man. The man put on his glasses and peered at the painting.

He seemed lost in contemplation.

"Excuse me," said DeKok after a while.

The man looked up.

"A lovely painting," he sighed. "Truly exquisite."

"Yes, it is," agreed DeKok, "but what about the costume?"

"Bohemia," said the small man.

"Is that part of Germany?"

"No, no," said the man, keeping his eyes on the painting. "It used to belong to Austria and then to Czecho-Slovakia. It's now part of what they call the Czech Republic."

20

DeKok was uncomfortable behind the wheel of the old police VW. He detested driving and by his own admission was probably the world's worst driver. Certainly the worst driver in Amsterdam. Peter Karstens was seated in the passenger seat and also looked uncomfortable. He also looked scared. He had heard the stories about DeKok's driving. The painting, wrapped in burlap, was on the back seat.

It had taken all of the DeKok's persuasion to induce the painter to cooperate. At first DeKok had thought about Little Lowee, or even Handie Henkie. But both were less suited to the mission than the painter.

Karstens held on with one hand on top of the seat belt and another on the grip on the dashboard.

"If I tell my friends about this," he complained, "they'll call me crazy."

"Then don't tell them," said DeKok curtly. He was sweating and devoted his full attention to driving the car.

Once outside of town DeKok cautiously increased speed. The little town of Dovecote, he thought, had played a more or less important part in the case from the beginning. Meanwhile he hoped that everything would succeed the way he had planned. It was, after all, a tremendous gamble. All he had to go on was his instinct and what he had learned about people. He hoped to exploit both this evening.

Four cars had been assigned to this particular action and that explained why DeKok was driving. Mark Stoops drove a nondescript Volvo and Vledder was in an equally nondescript Renault. Fred Prins was assigned to a Ford Taurus. Although he could not be sure of what was about to happen, DeKok felt certain that he had enough force to back him up. Actually, he thought, I am probably the weakest link of all. I can't even be sure of arriving in one piece.

But eventually they did reach their destination, although DeKok entered at least one one-way street from the wrong direction and at last parked crookedly half on and half off the sidewalk. He switched off the engine and turned toward Karstens.

"It's right around the corner. You have the address?"

"Yes," said Karstens, taking a deep breath now that the harrowing drive seemed to be over.

"Know your spiel?"

"I have," acted Karstens in an exaggerated tone of voice, "made this painting at the express instructions of Detective-Inspector DeKok of Warmoes Street station and he has ordered me to give it to you."

DeKok nodded.

"Change the tone, but the content is just right."

Karstens opened the car door.

"What if she won't accept the painting?"

DeKok smiled an encouraging smile.

"She will at least be curious."

The artist disappeared around the corner, the painting under one arm. DeKok remained in the car. He was tense. Within five minutes Karstens returned. Huffing and puffing, he slid into the seat.

"She's got it."

DeKok started up. He had promised to take the painter home. As they headed in the direction of the city, a walkie-talkie, which Vledder had thoughtfully placed on the back seat, crackled into life. The message was meant for all the other cars involved in the operation, but Vledder had made sure that DeKok would know what was happening. Vledder's voice came over the radio.

"Monika just left her building. She's carrying a large parcel and she's going to her car." Vledder voice was soft, but clear.

Karstens took his chance.

"You probably want to stay around, DeKok," he said. "Why don't you drop me off and I'll take a bus, or a cab, home."

DeKok gave him a grateful look, unaware that Karstens actually feared for his life in a car driven by the old sleuth.

As soon as he saw an opportunity, he drove to the side of the road and stopped. The artist shook his hand and quickly exited the car.

"Thanks," said DeKok.

"No problem," said Karstens, releasing a sigh of relief.

DeKok waved at his disappearing back and then decided to wait until there were further bulletins.

The walkie-talkie came to life again.

"She's driving toward the city, a red Mini Cooper." It was Vledder's voice.

"I've got it," said Stoops. Apparently there was a change in the pursuing cars. DeKok nodded approvingly. That's why he had requested the extra vehicles. It was important that Monika would have no suspicion of being followed.

"Hang on," said Prins. "She's changing direction. She's turning west toward Hilversum."

"Take it," said Stoops.

DeKok brought his own vehicle in motion. He thought he knew the general direction. Just past Hilversum started an area called the Veluwe, a large area almost in the center of Holland where the population was less dense than in the provinces along the coast. He listened to the various reports as they came over the radio on the back seat and soon discovered he had guessed right.

The reports continued, almost monotonously, until Stoops' voice suddenly broke in.

"She's driving into the driveway of a farm. I'm passing and setting up a roadblock."

"OK," sounded Vledder, "we see it. We'll take the other side."

Unless there was a back road out of the farm, it would be easy to block both sides off the narrow road that led to the farm. In this part of Holland there were just not too many super highways.

DeKok managed to get to the scene without major damage to himself, the car, or other drivers and stopped just behind the Taurus which Prins had been driving. Prins leaned against the car which was almost blocking the road.

"Still inside?" asked DeKok.

"Yes," answered Prins. "Vledder is just this side of the driveway and Stoops is ready to block the road from the other direction."

"All right," said DeKok. "Block the road. I'll join Vledder."

He walked towards Vledder while Prins pulled his car into the road in order to block both lanes. Stoops, upon radio instructions from Prins, did the same.

DeKok reached Vledder.

"Do you have one of those loudspeaker things?" asked DeKok.

"Yes." Vledder reached inside his car and handed DeKok a megaphone. DeKok took the instrument and after making sure that he knew how to operate it, he walked down the driveway toward the farm. His pulse rate was up and he was tense. He knew what the man he sought was capable of. At about twenty yards from the farmhouse he stopped and brought the megaphone to his mouth. He flipped the switch.

"Come out," he ordered, "with your hands in the air."

There was no sign of life from the farm.

DeKok repeated his order. The sound rolled over the flat landscape.

Suddenly there was another sound. With a bang the wooden barn doors flew open and a blue Jaguar suddenly leaped forward from the interior.

DeKok barely had time to jump out of the way as the powerful car roared up the driveway toward the road. It squashed the megaphone in passing. At the end of the driveway it made a skidding right turn and from his position DeKok could hear the gears shift. The engine roared and the car accelerated. Suddenly there was the squeal of brakes and the roaring of an engine which was forcibly down-shifted. Then there was the sound of a thunderclap, then a brief aftermath of tinkling glass and an eerie silence. The birds had stopped singing and no other traffic could be heard.

DeKok ran up the driveway in his waddling gait. Vledder and Prins were ahead of him. As they came nearer the scene of the accident, they saw Stoops come out of the ditch at the side of the road where he had beat a hasty retreat. The crumbled remains of the Jaguar were half buried into the side of what had once been a Volvo. Both cars were smashed beyond recognition.

Monika Buwalda had been thrown clear with the impact and was lying unconscious on the side of the road, just beyond

201

the crashed vehicles. The driver of the Jaguar was found in the middle of the road. Vledder was the first to reach the body.

"It's Peter Doon," he exclaimed.

The gray sleuth looked over the site of the ravage. There were pieces of cars everywhere and gasoline leaked from a ruptured tank.

Suddenly there was an explosion and soon the wreckage was engulfed in flames.

Peter Doon opened his eyes. With a desperate movement he managed to come to his feet and he staggered toward the burning vehicles. Yelling and screaming he leaned through the broken windows of the Jaguar and started to lift small, linen bags from the burning vehicle. Prins jumped after him. Near the fire the heat was almost unbearable. With a supreme effort, Prins managed to get hold of Doon's coat and, after a brief struggle, dragged him away from the fire. Unfortunately he had to drag him part of the way through the flaming gasoline on the ground. Most of Doon's clothes and his hair were on fire and Vledder quickly went back to his car. He ripped a blanket from the back seat and rolled the burning and screaming man in the blanket. Prins used his jacket to beat at the flames not covered by the blanket. Mercifully Doon lost consciousness while the detectives brought the rest of the flames under control.

Stoops came closer and while Vledder and Prins tried to make the burned man as comfortable as possible, they all watched as three million went up in flames.

21

The doorbell rang.

Mrs. DeKok opened the door. Vledder accompanied by Mark Stoops and Fred Prins stood on the stoop in front of the house. Mrs. DeKok greeted Vledder like an old friend. Vledder presented Mark Stoops who in turn presented Mrs. DeKok with a large bouquet of roses. Fred Prins grinned. He was almost as familiar with DeKok's ritual as Vledder.

"It's not my habit to present roses to women other than my wife," said Stoops, "but Vledder assured me it was a tradition."

Mrs. DeKok admired the flowers.

"They're beautiful," she assured him. "Very nice, indeed." She looked at Vledder. "Why don't you all come in," she invited.

Mrs. DeKok preceded the young Inspectors to the living room. Inspector DeKok was comfortably ensconced in a large easy chair. A venerable bottle of cognac and five snifters were placed within easy reach.

He waved at his colleagues and invited them to find seats. Mrs. DeKok excused herself and disappeared, with her roses, into the kitchen. DeKok started to pour. After a while Mrs. DeKok returned, several large platters of delicacies balanced in her hands. Prins jumped up and gave her a hand.

"Oh, thank you," she said, "just put them there on the sideboard and everybody can help themselves as needed."

She accepted a glass from her husband and sat down. DeKok raised his glass to her and then to the colleagues. Solemnly they all took their first sip. Mrs. DeKok put down her glass and went back into the kitchen. The cops talked about this and that. They talked about the reduction of the salaries in the police force and the limitations of overtime. DeKok said that he simply ignored filling out the paperwork for overtime and therefore never had any trouble. When Mrs. DeKok returned this time, she carried a large vase with the roses artfully arranged. She placed the vase on a table.

She resumed her seat.

"Very well," she said, "what's it all about?"

Vledder, who had been very quiet during the preceding, general conversation, suddenly burst out.

"Yes," he said, "how did you get Monika to leave her apartment and lead us directly to Peter Doon's hiding place?"

With a smile the gray sleuth pointed at the painting which, now provided with an appropriate frame, took pride of place over the fireplace.

"Happily I got it back. It was not damaged. It was leaning against the wall of the barn from which they made their escape." He told them how Karstens had delivered the painting and the message he had given.

"But you should know," he added, "that I had attached a little note to the painting. It read: *Greetings from Czecho-Slovakia* and I had signed Martin Muller's name to it. As I hoped, she panicked. The text indicated to her that I had solved the plot and knew who the killer was."

Vledder shook his head.

"Well, as far as I know, I knew the same things you did and I didn't see it." He sounded belligerent.

DeKok smiled and sipped from his cognac.

"But you did not commit the robbery," he said reasonably. He sat up in his chair and continued: "For Fred's and Mark's benefit, who were not involved in the beginning, I'll try to explain how it all fit together."

"I wish you would," grumbled Mrs. DeKok. She nodded approvingly when Stoops picked up one of the platters and, after helping himself, passed it around to the others.

"Well," began DeKok in his best lecturing voice, "Let me tell you that from the beginning I had my suspicions about the shadowy figure of Peter Shot. That is why I wanted to know if his fingerprints had shown up in the house of Mrs. Sloten. As it was, in retrospect the facts proved me right. There were no fingerprints belonging to Peter Shot, but there *were* a number of fingerprints belonging to Peter Doon." He grinned. "My suspicions regarding Monika Buwalda were reinforced when, the Peter Shot she had supposedly seen, walked in the wrong direction."

"Wrong direction?" asked Vledder.

DeKok nodded and looked at his glass. There was some cognac left and he drained the glass with a satisfied sigh. He reached for the bottle, but his wife put a restraining hand on his arm.

"No, you don't," she said severely. "Enough of these delaying tactics. First go on, then you can have another drink."

DeKok rolled his eyes, but placed his empty glass on a convenient side table and continued.

"Little Lowee told us that some 'friends' had seen Peter Shot, accompanied by a man and a woman, in Short King Street. They were going in the direction of Old Fort. When we later confronted Monika with this information, she said that Peter had had too much to drink and that they were taking him to his hotel on Martyrs Canal. Apart from the fact that there was no Peter

Shot, or anybody like him registered in a hotel on Martyrs Canal, something else was wrong. If you want to go to Martyrs Canal, you don't go in the direction of Old Fort and that's why they went in the 'wrong' direction. And that fits, because along Old Fort was the car they used to take the sick junkie to the farm. But more about that later."

"Why not now?" queried Vledder.

"Please," said DeKok, holding up a hand. "Let me continue in my own way."

"Oh, very well,"

"It all started when Monika took a temporary job at Houten & Busil. Later she thought that might get her into trouble, so she persuaded Peter Doon to break in and try to get her personnel records and destroy them. Which did not succeed, by the way. Anyway, Monika found the plan for a robbery in one of the drawers while she worked at the firm.

"So there *was* a plan?"

"Well, yes and no. It was more in the nature of a report. The firm that makes the armored cars had written a report about a robbery in France, where duplicate armored cars had been used. They routinely inform all their clients about anything that happens to affect the safety of their vehicles. If our dear, beloved Judge-Advocate hadn't interfered and prohibited us from talking to the directors, we would have found that out a lot sooner. Because of that restriction, this so-called plan remained shrouded in mystery and served to cloud the real issues."

He looked at his glass and then at his wife. She shook her head resolutely. He sighed with a smile.

"Well, Monika however, was obsessed by the plan and could not let go of the idea. She talked about it with Maria and as you know, she used the expression: *If you could only find a man who dared.* As you know, she found one."

Vledder nodded.

206

"But not at once," explained DeKok. "Monika had known Richard Sloten for some time, Slick Ricky, who was in the business of stealing expensive cars. They seemed to have had a an . . . eh . . . unbridled relationship, but when Monika proposed the plan of the robbery, Richard had second thoughts. He did not think it was his line. He just did not care for violence, as we know."

He stopped, as if to gather his thoughts. Before any of them could complain, he continued.

"Meanwhile Monika had met Peter Shot in a Disco. She was fascinated with his reputation, but she found him to be a bragging junkie, without any real substance as a possible partner. She had yet to meet the man who would meet her exacting standards. It turned out to be Peter Doon, the large, jovial long-distance trucker. It was Peter Doon's misfortune that he immediately, hopelessly fell in love. He was literally bewitched by Monika, who, as you know was an exceptionally beautiful woman, at least on the outside. She exudes a certain sensuality that can have a terrifying effect on men. I experienced that myself."

He glanced at Vledder who, blushing, nodded to himself. Mrs. DeKok noticed the exchange and smiled faintly.

"The effect on Peter Doon was so devastating that he became not just her partner, but her willing slave. He agreed to anything she said, agreed to anything she wanted as long as she would allow him to be with her, to adore her. She became his sole reason for living and nothing would satisfy him, unless he satisfied her first."

"That's crazy," said Stoops.

"Perhaps," agreed DeKok, "but history is full of some celebrated cases and I'm sure it happens more often than we think. It is not unusual. Some people fall in love, but other fall under a spell. In most cases, however, you wind up with what we call a devoted husband, or a devoted wife. It was Peter Doon's misfortune that he fell under the spell of a very ruthless woman. Whatever the reason, Peter Doon could not deny Monika anything. "

"Even murder?" asked Fred Prins.

"Yes. The original plan, the plan which involved duplicate trucks, was discarded. The cost of an extra truck would be too high and what could they do with it afterward? Monika had a better idea. For her plan it was necessary to get the cooperation of the driver, who had to deviate from his normal route. Well, Peter Doon talked Martin Muller into asking for a transfer to the armored cars. They needed two fast cars. Monika knew the answer to that as well and she brought Richard Sloten and Peter Doon together. Many meetings were arranged to work out all of the details and a number of them were held in Sloten's house. That is how Peter Doon got to know Mother Sloten. She is also the one who requested him to bring her a doll from Czecho-Slovakia, now the Czech Republic."

"The famous doll on the side table," interrupted Vledder.

"That doll was his downfall," said DeKok gravely.

Mark Stoops wanted clarification.

"But you two spent a lot of time trying to locate Peter Shot," he said. "I don't understand that. What did he have to do with anything?"

"Nothing," agreed DeKok, "that's to say . . . nothing with the robbery." he paused and gave his wife an apologetic look. "I've often said that if women have criminal tendencies, they are far more ruthless and devious than men. Monika had promised all participants an equal share of the loot, but she kept silent about the murders. Her game with Peter Shot is another example of her cunning. Peter Shot was to be the scapegoat. In addition, Peter Shot provided the weapon that was later used to do the killing."

Stoops jumped up.

"I told you that serpent thought too much of herself."

DeKok laughed at the reaction.

"I have earned another drink," he said.

"Yes," his wife agreed. Then, while DeKok poured another round, she directed Fred Prins to hand round one of the platters. The Dutch seem incapable of drinking alcohol without snacking. While they all nibbled contentedly, DeKok took a sip from his drink.

"Go on, Jurriaan," she urged. Stoops and Prins looked up. They had not known DeKok's Christian name.

"With some savings Monika and Peter Doon had bought an option on an old farm. They intended to live there . . . after the furor had died down. Monika was not planning on a life as a fugitive. She realized full well that the police wouldn't rest until it had arrested the perpetrators of the robbery, especially since it involved a murder. Well, that was no problem for somebody as ruthless as she. She was ready to deliver her scapegoat . . . Peter Shot."

Vledder grinned, somewhat abashed.

"She almost succeeded."

"Yes, but almost only counts in 'Horseshoes' or hand grenades," said DeKok.

"None of that," admonished Mrs. DeKok, who knew her husband's penchant for straying into obscure references and then taking an inordinate delight in explaining them.

"All right, all right. One night they picked up Peter Shot in the street somewhere. Peter was already suffering from the complications caused by the poisoned heroin . . . something Monika did not know. She really thought he had too much to drink that night. Together with Peter Doon she abducted him and kept him prisoner on the farm. Carmen Manouskicheck was right. Peter had disappeared. Meanwhile the last details of the robbery were nailed down. At the express orders from Monika, Peter Doon first killed Martin Muller and then Richard Sloten. When she was in the station to tell us about her 'fiancee,' she already knew that Peter Doon was on the way to Richard's mother."

Mrs. DeKok shivered.

"It's diabolical," she muttered.

DeKok took a deep breath.

"Monika Buwalda didn't want any witnesses . . . nobody who could later blackmail her. All participants had to be killed. The last murder was the killing of Peter Shot. That happened on the farm. They transported the corpse back to Amsterdam and arranged for an apparent death by overdose."

"How could that boy do it?" asked Mrs. DeKok, shaking her head.

"Peter Doon, you mean?"

"Yes."

DeKok gestured vaguely.

"I talked with him for a long time. He's still in the special burn unit at Wilhelmina Hospital. They expect him to die before the week is out. He's been too severely burned. The remarkable thing is that he is lucid and able to talk about his action in a rational and reasonable way. His love for Monika did indeed manifest itself in a slavish submission. It was, so he said, as if he had no will of his own. Ever since he met her he was on a different plane, an exalted plane . . . in ecstasy, he said. He lived to please her and the prospect of all that money seemed to strengthen his desires. All his killings were committed as if he was a spectator. He was following the orders of his own particular goddess and nothing else seemed to matter."

Prins looked doubtful.

"Murder in ecstasy? Is that possible?"

"When my love swears that she is made of truth, I do believe her, though I know she lies," said Mrs. DeKok.

"You see," smiled DeKok.

"Eh . . . what's that?" asked Vledder.

"One of Shakespeare's sonnets," explained Mrs. DeKok. "You see, the Bard also knew about men being besotted by women."

"It's sick," said Prins.

"No, it's human," said DeKok. "That he had not completely lost his senses, is witnessed by the fact that he panicked after he had killed Mrs. Sloten. He looked around for traces of his presence and spotted the doll. That's why he removed it. Obviously he thought it was the only thing that could link him to the killings. In a sense he was right, although not the way he expected."

"And what about Ria Muller and Houten?" Stoops wanted to know.

"Well, the relationship is pretty much according to what Ria told us. Houten may have liked to go further, but Ria just wasn't interested. Of course," he added, "that did not prevent her from using Houten's feelings for her to get her husband transferred. As for Houten, I don't know, but I am certain Ria will not marry him. He will always be a reminder of her dead husband."

DeKok leaned back and savored his cognac. There was silence in the room until Prins spoke up.

"When are you arresting Monika?" he asked.

DeKok pursed his lips.

"Sometimes, Fred," he said slowly, "sometimes it seems that our earthly justice is no longer important. Monika Buwalda will never walk again. Her hips were almost completely pulverized. She will spend the rest of her life in a wheel chair."

211

About the Author:

Albert Cornelis Baantjer (BAANTJER) first appeared on the American literary scene in September, 1992 with "DeKok and Murder on the Menu". He was a member of the Amsterdam Municipal Police force for more than 38 years and for more than 25 years he worked Homicide out of the ancient police station at 48 Warmoes Street, on the edge of Amsterdam's Red Light District. The average tenure of an officer in "the busiest police station of Europe" is about five years. Baantjer stayed until his retirement.

His appeal in the United States has been instantaneous and praise for his work has been universal. "If there could be another Maigret-like police detective, he might well be Detective-Inspector DeKok of the Amsterdam police," according to *Bruce Cassiday* of the International Association of Crime Writers. "It's easy to understand the appeal of Amsterdam police detective DeKok," writes *Charles Solomon* of the Los Angeles Times. Baantjer has been described as "a Dutch Conan Doyle" (Publishers Weekly) and has been called "a new major voice in crime fiction in America" (*Ray B. Browne*, CLUES: A Journal of Detection).

Perhaps part of the appeal is because much of Baantjer's fiction is based on real-life (or death) situations encountered during his long police career. He writes with the authority of an expert and with the compassion of a person who has seen too much suffering. He's been there.

The critics and the public have been quick to appreciate the charm and the allure of Baantjer's work. Seven "DeKok's" have been used by the (Dutch) Reader's Digest in their series of condensed books (called "Best Books" in Holland). In his native Holland, with a population of less than 15 million people, Baantjer has sold more than 5 million books and according to the Netherlands Library Information Service, a Baantjer/DeKok is checked out of a library more than 700,000 times per year.

American reviews suggest that Baantjer may become as popular in English as he is already in Dutch.

The following story appeared in a collection of eight short stories by Baantjer, published on the occasion of the 50th Anniversary of Baantjer's Dutch Publisher. Original Copy-Right (1996) by Uitgeverij De Fontein, Baarn, Netherlands.

DeKok and . . . I

It was inevitable. Sooner or later DeKok would meet ex-Inspector Baantjer. It happened during a clammy, overcast night at the police station in Warmoes Street. The bleak ceiling lights in the station house hummed and the muted sounds of the Quarter penetrated into the detective room.

DeKok gave Baantjer a searching look.

"So, you're the guy who's always writing about me."

Baantjer nodded resignedly.

"I have followed your career very closely and let me add that I admire you greatly."

DeKok snorted.

"That stinks."

Baantjer looked surprised.

"What do you mean . . . stinks?"

DeKok grinned a crooked grin.

"It's just pure self-love. Admiration for me, means admiration for yourself."

Baantjer pulled out his lower lip and let it plop back.

"My compliments . . . a sharp observation."

DeKok shook his head, looking sad.

"Wrong again. That compliment to me . . . is a compliment to yourself. I only exist because of you."

"And you're at peace with that?"

DeKok shrugged his shoulders.

"I do have a few reservations."

"Speak up."

"Why do I always have such tired feet?"

Baantjer laughed wholeheartedly.

"Because they trouble me, too."

DeKok growled and rubbed his tender calves.

"That's not something to laugh about. You could have changed me, you know. Make me someone different, younger, more energetic, a real hero with an athletic figure."

"Would you have liked that?"

DeKok ignored the question. For some time he stared into the distance. Then his eyebrows flickered briefly out of focus and he returned to his visitor.

"Ach," he said, slowly. "I don't really know. But I do believe that you torture me unnecessarily from an erotic point of view."

"How's that?"

"You keep bringing in these beautiful, blonde women. For most literature heroes that means immediately the start of a romantic adventure. But me, me . . . you never let me touch anything, never let me get close."

"Well, we do happen to be blessed with an abundance of beautiful, blonde women. As for the touching, getting close as you call it, would you have liked that?"

A smile fled across DeKok's face.

"The thought makes me happy."

Baantjer moved in his chair.

"Who knows what sort of erotic adventures I might allow you in the future. Otherwise . . . any more complaints?"

"I'm so . . . so *square*."

Baantjer frowned.

"That is bad?"

"One sometimes talks about it in a sneering, almost scornful way."

"Who does?"

DeKok pursed his lips.

"There are people who find the concept of 'Law and Order' a bit scary."

Baantjer became angry and it showed in his voice.

"You know what 'Law and Order' means to me?" he asked heatedly, gesturing violently. "Not much more than that my old mother, who's nearly eighty, can take a quiet stroll around the block of an evening, without having to worry about being robbed, or worse. And also," he continued, less loudly, but just as passionately, "that my 17-year old niece can walk home after a party, without being molested."

DeKok looked surprised.

"I had not expected that much emotion from you."

Baantjer pressed his lips together. Then he relented.

"That emotion always comes to the fore when I think about the well being of the average citizen."

"And who is the average citizen?"

"Those are hard-working, men and women of good will . . . fathers and housewives who make sure to be home before dark and then seek protection behind double-locked doors and a bar across the back door."

DeKok laughed loudly and with obvious pleasure.

"And you . . . a guy like you is my spiritual father?"

Baantjer looked unsure of himself.

"Ridiculous?" he asked, tentatively.

DeKok shook his head.

"You're a sad example of a knight in shining armor."

Baantjer sighed.

"Perhaps you're right . . . a sad knight. After all, every cop is some sort of Don Quichote. He, or she, fights against crime and that is . . . that is tilting at windmills. The safety in the streets that a cop strives after, is just as unreachable as the beautiful Dulcinea. And the upstanding citizen, in whose service the cops fight, is . . . like Sancho Panza, more concerned with a full belly."

The shrill sound of the phone broke the silence between them.

Baantjer lifted the receiver from the hook and listened. Then he handed the phone to DeKok.

"It's for you . . . the Watch Commander, downstairs."

DeKok listened for a while, then he replaced the receiver.

"Something up?" asked Baantjer.

"They just found the corpse of a young woman."

"Where?"

"A small hotel on Rear Fort Canal. The constables suspect a crime. The circumstances seem peculiar."

DeKok lifted his legs and placed them on his desk.

"Aren't you going?" asked Baantjer.

"Vledder is already on the way. If he needs me, he'll call me."

"What about Vledder?"

DeKok smiled.

"A man out of a thousand. I could not have imagined a better assistant."

Baantjer looked thoughtful.

"Some people think he's a bit young and impulsive . . . dumb even. I worry about that. But after he 'paid his dues' with the Amsterdam Police, he was promoted to CI (Central Intelligence) in The Hague and there he's been promoted to Commissaris."

DeKok looked at Baantjer.

"And what about this Commissaris Buitendam, with whom I'm always at odds in *your* books?"

Baantjer smiled.

"That is an ex-Commissaris of the Amsterdam Police, Mr. W.T.G.A. Binnendijk (*inner dike*, trans.) who certainly could handle his personnel a lot better that your fictitious boss."

"You mess around a lot with names, don't you. Is there a system? Binnendijk (*inner dike*) becomes Buitendam (*outer dam*, trans.). What about Dr. Rusteloos (*restless*, trans.) . . . why is that?"

Baantjer's eyes twinkled.

"Do you remember Dr. Zeldenrust (*seldom rest*, trans.)?"

DeKok nodded thoughtfully.

"Don't worry too much about it," added Baantjer, "you should see what they do with the names in the American translations. According to the publisher there, if the names were left untranslated, the books would soon resemble Russian novels, requiring the reader to continually flip back and forth to keep track of the names."

"Oh, how do they solve that?"

"They simplify the names. *Van der's-Gravezande* becomes *Graven*. *Achtervoorburgwal* becomes *Rear Fort Canal* and so on."

"Clever," grunted DeKok. Then he asked: "How do they do that in the Russian translations?"

"I don't know," confessed Baantjer, "I don't read Russian. But I did notice that in the Korean translations, whenever a name is used for the first time, they put it in parenthesis in roman letter behind the pictograph. From then on, they apparently only use the pictographs." He shrugged. "The words in parenthesis were the only parts I could read in the Korean translations."

Again DeKok nodded to himself

"And what about all those crimes?" he asked after a long pause. "All those complicated murders you had me solve . . . were those real?"

Baantjer rubbed his graying hair. The he spoke.

"They were real, yes," he said, hesitantly. "Just as real and true as you, DeKok. Because, believe me, you exist. As long as there is an Amsterdam and there are people who, despite everything, are willing to take on the heavy task of the police."

The phone rang again.

This time DeKok lifted the receiver and listened. Almost immediately he replaced the receiver and walked over to the peg.

"It was young Vledder," he explained. "It's murder."

"The young woman in the hotel?"

"Strangled."

Both men pulled on their raincoats and placed almost identical, decrepit little hats on their heads. Slowly they descended the stairs.

They left the old, ancient police station and walked in the direction of Rear Fort Canal. Baantjer, impatient, a little ahead and DeKok, more leisurely, slightly behind.

As usual, crowds gathered in front of the sex-shops windows and lined up in front of the sex theaters. Men spoke loudly and in many languages. Women giggled and sniggered.

A van from the Coroner's Office was parked in front of the small hotel. A young constable pointed the way.

"She's on the second floor . . . room six."

They climbed the creaking, winding stairs. Vledder was waiting for them upstairs. Baantjer reached for his hand and introduced himself. The young inspector spoke surly.

"I'd rather you weren't here, we get too many people messing up the crime scene as it is."

Baantjer ignored the remark. Together with DeKok he observed the room. The first thing he noticed was a slogan on the wall: *God is Love*. The word "Love" had been crossed off with a thick line of red lipstick. On a white-painted chair were clothes, neatly folded on the seat, or draped over the back. A skirt. a sweater, a minuscule brassiere. On a small table against the wall were her few possessions. A lipstick, a compact, a few wrinkled dollar bills and some Dutch currency. Baantjer wondered if she had crossed off the word *Love*. But the lipstick was a different color.

The young woman was situated diagonally across the bed. Nude. Her head hung down over one edge. The strangulation marks on her neck were clearly visible.

DeKok motioned toward the attendants. They placed the body into the body bag and strapped it to the stretcher.

Baantjer watched.

"Has the Coroner been already?"

DeKok nodded.

"Vledder spoke with him. She's been strangled with bare hands."

After the body had been removed, the two old men went back downstairs. It had become chillier and a light drizzle had started to fall. Baantjer and DeKok pulled up the collars of their coats.

DeKok looked at Vledder.

"You have her name?"

The young Inspector nodded.

"A prostitute. Came from Rotterdam. I also have the name of her last client."

DeKok smiled.

"Very good. Look around, just to make sure. Baantjer and I are going back to the station house."

They walked away . . . both of them in an old raincoat . . . both of them with an old, decrepit little hat on their heads. The drizzle changed to fog and long swirls of vapor rose from the canal to obscure the contours of the narrow bridge across from Stove Alley. Vledder watched them leave. Suddenly something strange seemed to happen. The blurry figures seemed to come closer together . . . merged into one. What was left was a coat, a little hat.

Only DeKok crossed the bridge.

Murder in Amsterdam
Baantjer

The two very first "DeKok" stories for the first time in a single volume, containing *DeKok and the Sunday Strangler* and *DeKok and the Corpse on Christmas Eve.*

First American edition of these European
Best-Sellers in a single volume.
Second Printing

From critical reviews of **Murder in Amsterdam**:

If there could be another Maigret-like police detective, he might well be Detective-Inspector DeKok of the Amsterdam police. Similarities to Simenon abound in any critical judgement of Baantjer's work (*Bruce Cassiday*, **International Association of Crime Writers**); The two novellas make an irresistible case for the popularity of the Dutch author. DeKok's maverick personality certainly makes him a compassionate judge of other outsiders and an astute analyst of antisocial behavior (*Marilyn Stasio*, **The New York Times Book Review**); Both stories are very easy to take (**Kirkus Reviews**); Inspector DeKok is part Columbo, part Clouseau, part genius, and part imp. Baantjer has managed to create a figure hapless and honorable, bozoesque and brilliant, but most importantly, a body for whom the reader finds compassion (*Steven Rosen*, **West Coast Review of Books**); Readers of this book will understand why the author is so popular in Holland. His DeKok is a complex, fascinating individual (*Ray Browne*, **CLUES: A Journal of Detection**); This first translation of Baantjer's work into English supports the mystery writer's reputation in his native Holland as a Dutch Conan Doyle. His knowledge of esoterica rivals that of Holmes, but Baantjer wisely uses such trivia infrequently, his main interests clearly being detective work, characterization and moral complexity (**Publishers Weekly**).

ISBN: 1-881164-00-4
LCCN: 96-36722
$9.95

The Cop Was White As Snow

Joyce Spizer

THE COP'S SUICIDE on a lonely beach confirmed his guilt. He had been skimming cocaine from police impounds and selling it to drug dealers to support his own habit and a growing taste for luxury. But he was Mel's Dad, and she was not about to accept this for a minute. Her Dad was no dirty cop!

THE COP WAS WHITE AS SNOW is a fast read. Spizer does a good job of keeping the action coming. Her insight as an investigator resonates throughout the book.
—Barbara Seranell, author of No Human Involved

JOYCE SPIZER is the shamus she writes about. The novels in the Harbour Pointe Mystery Series are fictionalized accounts of cases she has investigated. A member of Sisters in Crime, she hobnobs regularly with other mystery writers. She lives in Southern California with her husband and co-investigator, Harold.

SBN 1-886411-83-7
LCCN: 97-39430
$10.95

TWISTED

CAHROUL CRAMER

As the Chief of Homicide, the newly promoted Lieutenant Turner Fleece was expected to act as a supervisor and not as an investigator. But when an up and coming recording artist and her lover are brutally murdered in the woman's San Francisco home, the thrill of the hunt is more than Fleece can resist. He is seductively led through a maze of deceit and corruption. And at the very moment when it seems he has untangled the mystery, he realizes it has only become more twisted.

SBN 1-886411-82-9
LCCN: 97-42995
$9.95

ALSO FROM INTERCONTINENTAL PUBLISHING:

The "DeKok" series by Baantjer.

If there could be another Maigret-like police detective, he might well be Detective-Inspector DeKok of the Amsterdam police. Similarities to Simenon abound in any critical judgement of Baantjer's work (***Bruce Cassiday*, International Association of Crime Writers**); DeKok's maverick personality certainly makes him a compassionate judge of other outsiders and an astute analyst of antisocial behavior (***Marilyn Stasio*, The New York Times Book Review**); DeKok is part Columbo, part Clouseau, part genius, and part imp. (***Steven Rosen*, West Coast Review of Books**); It's easy to understand the appeal of Amsterdam police detective DeKok (***Charles Solomon*, Los Angeles Times**); DeKok is a careful, compassionate policeman in the tradition of Maigret (**Library Journal**); This series is the answer to an insomniac's worst fears (***Robin W. Winks*, The Boston Globe**).

The following Baantjer/DeKok books are currently in print:

MURDER IN AMSTERDAM (contains complete text of *DeKok and the Sunday Strangler* and *DeKok and the Corpse on Christmas Eve*);
DEKOK AND THE SOMBER NUDE
DEKOK AND THE DEAD HARLEQUIN
DEKOK AND THE SORROWING TOMCAT
DEKOK AND THE DISILLUSIONED CORPSE
DEKOK AND THE CAREFUL KILLER
DEKOK AND THE ROMANTIC MURDER
DEKOK AND THE DYING STROLLER
DEKOK AND THE CORPSE AT THE CHURCH WALL
DEKOK AND THE DANCING DEATH
DEKOK AND THE NAKED LADY
DEKOK AND THE BROTHERS OF THE EASY DEATH
DEKOK AND THE DEADLY ACCORD
DEKOK AND MURDER IN SEANCE
DEKOK AND MURDER IN ECSTASY
DEKOK AND MURDER ON THE MENU.

Available soon: **DeKok and the Begging Death; DeKok and the Geese of Death** and more . . . Additional titles published regularly.

Available in your bookstore. U.S. distribution by IPG, Chicago, IL.